In Honor of The Jasper Gulch Centennial, You Are Cordially Invited to Attend the World's Largest Old-Tyme Wedding

One hundred brides and grooms to celebrate one hundred years of history! Folks are coming from all over to see this romantic spectacle. Everyone seems happy—except perhaps perpetual bridesmaid Katie Archer. She's starting to regret her decision to come to Jasper Gulch to watch her sister wed….

For better or worse, she's agreed to help Cord Shaw, the mayor's son, pull off the perfect wedding ceremony. But we suspect that Katie is harboring her own secret wish involving a tuxedo and a long white gown. Things are about to get *very* complicated—and you've got the best seat in the house to watch it all unfold. Something old, something new, something borrowed…and you! Stay tuned for an Old West wedding you will never forget!

* * *

Big Sky Centennial:
A small town rich in history…and love.

Her Montana Cowboy by Valerie Hansen—*July 2014*
His Montana Sweetheart by Ruth Logan Herne—*August 2014*
Her Montana Twins by Carolyne Aarsen—*September 2014*
His Montana Bride by Brenda Minton—*October 2014*
His Montana Homecoming by Jenna Mindel—*November 2014*
Her Montana Christmas by Arlene James—*December 2014*

Books by Brenda Minton

Love Inspired

Trusting Him
His Little Cowgirl
A Cowboy's Heart
The Cowboy Next Door
Rekindled Hearts
Blessings of the Season
"The Christmas Letter"
Jenna's Cowboy Hero
The Cowboy's Courtship
The Cowboy's Sweetheart
Thanksgiving Groom
The Cowboy's Family
The Cowboy's Homecoming
Christmas Gifts
*"Her Christmas Cowboy"
**The Cowboy's Holiday Blessing*
**The Bull Rider's Baby*
**The Rancher's Secret Wife*
**The Cowboy's Healing Ways*
**The Cowboy Lawman*
The Boss's Bride
**The Cowboy's Christmas Courtship*
**The Cowboy's Reunited Family*
**Single Dad Cowboy*
His Montana Bride

*Cooper Creek

BRENDA MINTON

started creating stories to entertain herself during hour-long rides on the school bus. In high school she wrote romance novels to entertain her friends. The dream grew and so did her aspirations to become an author. She started with notebooks, handwritten manuscripts and characters who refused to go away until their stories were told. Eventually she put away the pen and paper and got down to business with the computer. The journey took a few years, with some encouragement and rejection along the way—as well as a lot of stubbornness on her part. In 2006 her dream to write for Love Inspired Books came true. Brenda lives in the rural Ozarks with her husband, three kids and an abundance of cats and dogs. She enjoys a chaotic life that she wouldn't trade for anything—except, on occasion, a beach house in Texas. You can stop by and visit at her website, www.brendaminton.net.

His Montana Bride

Brenda Minton

Special thanks and acknowledgment to Brenda Minton for her contribution to the Big Sky Centennial miniseries.

Recycling programs for this product may not exist in your area.

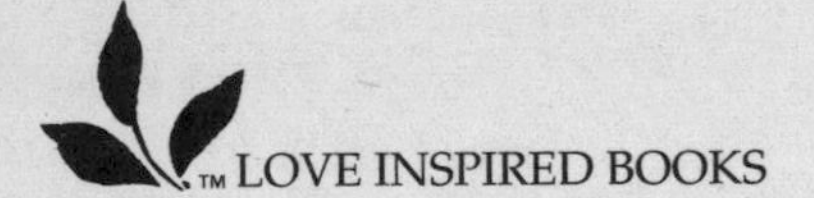

ISBN-13: 978-0-373-81792-4

HIS MONTANA BRIDE

This edition published by arrangement with Love Inspired Books.

www.Harlequin.com

Printed in U.S.A.

Ask, and it shall be given you; seek,
and ye shall find; knock, and it shall be opened unto you.
—*Matthew* 7:7

To the wonderful ladies who made working on this continuity such a pleasure: Valerie Hansen, Carolyne Aarsen, Ruth Logan Herne, Jenna Mindel and Arlene James. Your support and prayers have meant so much to me. And to our editor, Shana Asaro, for making it a great project to work on.

Chapter One

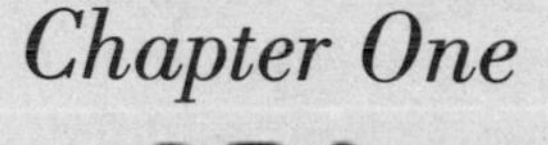

Jasper Gulch Welcomes You To the World's Largest Old Tyme Wedding. The banner was stretched across one wall of the Jasper Gulch, Montana, festival hall at the fairgrounds. The town was celebrating its centennial and for some reason, a hundred years meant a hundred brides and grooms. Or at least that was someone's opinion. Katie Archer wasn't one of the brides. Instead, she stood on the sidelines, the sister of a bride, as well as a potential bridesmaid. It was the place where she felt comfortable and where she'd spent most of her life—standing in the shadow of her older sister, Gwen.

Gwen was beautiful, intelligent, gifted and so many other positive adjectives, but she was also unfailingly kind. And Katie was loyal. When Gwen had asked her to make this trip, Katie hadn't been able to refuse, even though she knew

Gwen would have to leave at times. Katie had taken vacation from her job in Missoula, packed a bag and climbed into the backseat of Jeffrey's Land Rover, Jeffrey behind the wheel, Gwen in the passenger seat. Jeffrey Parker, the groom, was an orthopedic surgeon originally from Denver but now practicing in Missoula. The two had met when Gwen started her residency.

They had arrived in the small town of Jasper Gulch, Montana, earlier in the day. There had been time to take a tour of the town, find the Shaw ranch where they would be staying during the month of October while they prepared for the wedding, and then they'd headed for the fairgrounds where the engaged couples would be treated to a prewedding reception.

Since arriving at the cavernous, slightly drafty building, Katie had watched as Gwen and her fiancé, better known as Dr. Jeff, got the royal treatment. Even from a distance Katie could see that her sister and Jeff were in love. And they looked beautiful together, like the power couple they were. Gwen looked stunning with her dark hair in a jeweled clip, a shimmering red dress that suited her slim frame and her makeup applied perfectly.

Gwen and Katie were complete opposites in every way.

After a lifetime of being compared to Gwen,

somewhere along the way Katie had learned to smile and let it go. She would never be the honors student. She would never be the perfect daughter. She would always be Katie, the redhead with a penchant for flirting just to get noticed.

Anything to get noticed.

At least she had been that person. In the last two years she had learned to accept herself, the person God had created. She'd stopped the continuous race to find someone to love and to love her. She'd learned to love herself.

She shifted from foot to high-heeled foot and watched the crowds, the couples and the townspeople. The Shaws, their hosts while in Jasper Gulch, were interesting. Jackson Shaw and his wife, Nadine, were the patriarch and matriarch of the family and the community. Mayor Jackson Shaw, tall and distinguished and definitely a Montana rancher, was in charge. His wife stayed close to his side.

But there was tension. Katie had watched the couple share a few looks that she thought meant a lot more than "isn't this a great event." Having survived her parents' rocky marriage, she knew the signs of a couple not in agreement. She didn't think the tension was limited to the Shaw family, either. She got the feeling the community of Jasper Gulch was packing a lot of hope into this six-month centennial celebration.

It seemed a few people wanted to keep the community just the way it was, cut off from the rest of Montana with just one road in and out.

Katie stopped to look at a bulletin board with old photos of the town and a few new photographs, as well as schedules for coming events and plans for improvement. There was a picture of the Beaver Creek bridge as it stood today and a photograph from the town's heyday. There were pictures of the main street through town with old automobiles parked in front of stores that were no longer in business. Jasper Gulch was like so many towns around the country. It had served its purpose years ago, long before airlines, technology and chain stores. Now it struggled to stay alive. Being secluded as it was probably worked in favor of the businesses that were still in operation.

Even with its struggles, it would have been nice to grow up in a town like this, with a family that went to church, with people who knew your name. But she hadn't. She slipped away from the memorabilia, some of which would be put in the new museum, if it ever got built.

Katie had spent her younger years in San Diego but had grown up in Missoula in a subdivision with neighbors she barely knew. Her parents had both worked long hours. Sunday had been the day of rest, but not a day for church. The four Archers had spent little time together.

Katie had dreamed of a place like this, a small town situated in a valley surrounded by mountains and with a deep blue sky that seemed to go on forever. The acres of ranch land, the surrounding mountains and the sparkling, clear streams. Who wouldn't want to call this home and preserve it for future generations?

With a cup of hot cider from the refreshment table, she sank onto a folding chair and watched the crowds. From across the room an elderly man smiled her way. She smiled back and he tipped his hat. She had been introduced to him earlier and thought his name might be Rusty. He'd played baseball as a youngster and he was nearly as old as Jasper Gulch, he'd informed her.

Her gaze moved from the aging ball player and landed on Cord Shaw, son of Jackson and Nadine. She'd met him at the Shaw ranch, but briefly. The tall, sun-tanned cowboy with the dark wavy hair hadn't stayed long at the main ranch house. He'd greeted their guests, thanked them for participating in the wedding and then he'd made excuses about work at his own place.

Typical of most of the men here, Cord wore jeans and a dark sport coat over a button-down shirt. His cowboy hat was black, matching his jacket. He turned and smiled. Maybe at her. Probably not. Gwen had moved into the spotlight and men always smiled at Gwen. Men, women, babies and the elderly. They couldn't help it. Gwen was the flame and everyone around her a moth.

"Those Shaw men, they sure are hot, aren't they?"

The statement took her by surprise. She turned and smiled at the young woman who had taken the seat next to hers. The girl was pretty, maybe late teens, and definitely too made up. Her clothes were too loud, her hair too sleek. Katie smiled at her and refrained from commenting on the Shaw men.

"I'm sorry?" What else could a woman say when caught staring at a man?

The younger woman nodded in the direction of Cord Shaw.

"Cord Shaw, he's the older brother. By the way, I'm Lilibeth Shoemaker." She held out a well-manicured hand. "I've lived here my whole life, so I know everyone."

"I see." Katie continued to watch Cord Shaw. He was a gentleman. It was obvious in the way he moved through the crowd, the respect he showed, the way he stopped to listen to his mother.

She didn't meet men like him in Missoula. They probably existed, but they didn't run in her circle. She wished they did. No, she took that back. She'd given up on romance. Men wanted her for a friend because she was fun and easy to be around. She wasn't the woman they dated or thought about marrying. She was too tall, too opinionated, too much.

"That's his brother Austin." Lilibeth Shoemaker broke in to Katie's thoughts once more with her sharp-edged observations and pointed to another cowboy threading his way through the crowd. She didn't remember meeting him.

"I don't think I've met him." Katie didn't know what else to say. The young woman at her side didn't seem to care.

"It's a shame that Cord won't ever get married. Burn him once, shame on you. Burn him twice, well, I don't know the rest of that, but I guess being burned makes a man a little nervous around the fire."

"Gotcha." Katie smiled at the teenager. She got the feeling Lilibeth needed friends.

She remembered now, meeting another young woman named Shoemaker, but that one had been a little older than Lilibeth and maybe a little more polished around the edges. She and Lilibeth had something in common. They lived in the shadows of older siblings.

"Where are you from?"

Katie smiled at the girl. "I'm from Missoula."

"I'd love to live in the city. All the lights and noise and people. What do you do?"

People always wanted what they didn't have. Katie glanced around the crowd, not really looking for a way out, just looking. "I'm an assistant manager of a clothing store."

"Oh." Lilibeth looked down at her spiky-heeled, bright red pumps. "I've always wanted to do something in fashion. I'd like to be a model. But I can't even win a beauty pageant in Jasper Gulch, so figure the odds."

"Maybe someday," Katie offered with what she hoped was an encouraging tone. "You know, modeling and beauty pageants aren't really the same."

Lilibeth shrugged. "Yeah, maybe. I don't know. I'd probably leave tomorrow if I could. People always think I'm up to something."

Katie only nodded because the conversation seemed too personal for strangers. She sympathized, though, because she knew how it felt to be the younger sister, always in trouble. Words of wisdom evaded her. What did she tell a young woman that even a newcomer like herself had heard whispers about? Small talk at the party had included a discussion of the time capsule that seemed to be missing.

And then Gwen was heading her way, waving and smiling. Katie shot a look past her sister to Jeffrey and the man at his side. She got a tangled feeling in the pit of her stomach. What had made her think this trip with Gwen would be a good idea? Had she really thought it would be easy, to come here and watch her sister get married, to be the bridesmaid again?

At least this time she didn't have feelings, other than the brotherly kind, for the groom.

Cord Shaw listened to the doctor, groom to one of their brides, tell him about his practice in Missoula. As he listened to Dr. Jeff, Cord's attention wandered through the crowd. He was looking for Helen Avery, the wedding coordinator. She should have been here by now, seeing to the needs of their couples, tying up loose ends, making sure everyone had what they needed to go forward with the wedding. Instead, she was missing in action. Again. It wasn't the first time she'd been late or a no-show.

And that left this mess of a wedding on his shoulders. He was the last guy who wanted to plan weddings. He loved his parents and would do anything for his dad, but maybe this had gone too far.

Finally.

He caught sight of his little sister Julie and her fiancé, Ryan Travers. His sister's auburn curls framed her face. And even though this event was supposedly evening dress, or the Jasper Gulch version of evening attire, Julie wore a long sweater made with her wool, leggings, boots and a scarf around her neck. He shook his head and refocused on Dr. Jeff, who was still talking about his practice.

"Oh, Gwen wants you to meet her sister." Dr. Jeff took a break to indicate his fiancée and the woman she was dragging toward them.

The woman didn't look at all like Gwen Archer. The sister was tall, with brilliant red hair held in a clasp at the back of her head. A few stray curls had come loose and framed her face. A porcelain-doll face was his first thought. One of his sisters had collected those dolls and she'd had one with a perky nose, high cheekbones and creamy skin. But then he realized the sister of Gwen Archer had somewhat more defined features than those dolls. She was the exact opposite of her dark-haired, petite sister. Rose Red and Snow White came to mind as he looked at the Archers.

The bride's sister wore a black dress with a flimsy black sweater that shouldn't even have been called a sweater in his opinion. She said something to her sister and then she looked up, smiling at him, her green eyes flashing a warning. She had No Trespassing written all over her face. This was not a woman wanting to be fixed up, introduced or paired off.

He breathed a sigh of relief.

"Cord Shaw, this is my sister, Katie Archer." Gwen held her sister's arm and he noticed the firm set of the younger woman's back. With her green eyes she could have been a cat about to scratch someone.

"Pleased to meet you, Miss Archer." He held out a hand, forcing her to make the next move even if she didn't want to. She hesitated and he felt a little bit guilty for forcing her hand, so to speak.

After the moment of hesitation, she reached and he took her hand in his. His attention focused on the jangle of silver bracelets around her wrist. When he looked up, she was watching him, her smile soft but genuine.

"Mr. Shaw, I believe we were already introduced."

Had they been? He tried to remember but couldn't. "I'm sorry."

"Don't be." But the look in her eyes bothered him. Something about that look said she expected to be forgotten. And Cord couldn't imagine anyone forgetting this woman. Even a confirmed bachelor like himself wasn't immune to a beautiful woman. He just knew to avoid them for all he was worth.

Gwen Archer had an arm around her sister's waist, but her dark eyes were on him. It would have been a good time to walk away, but curiosity kept him standing in front of them.

"I'm afraid Jeff and I are going to have to leave tonight. We were planning to stay at the ranch until Monday or Tuesday, but Jeffrey got a call and they need him in Missoula. I have to ride back with him so I can be at work Wednesday. I'm a resident at the same hospital. Your parents would have given Katie a ride, but their truck is full. Your dad said to see if you could give her a ride."

Yes, that was the moment he should have seen coming. With all this romance in the air, people were going to get crazy and start expecting everyone to want to join in the fun. His dad had already been on the matchmaking crusade with his sisters. Cord managed an easy smile and opened his mouth to object.

"I can go home with you, Gwen. I don't think I need to be here. I'm just the bridesmaid." Katie shot him an apologetic look and he realized they were definitely kindred spirits.

Gwen's eyes narrowed. She looked at Dr. Jeff, then at Cord and finally back to her sister. "You have to stay. They're going to start planning the wedding procession, picking flowers and even cakes. If I can't get back here in time, I'll need you here to stand in for me. You, more than anyone, will know what I want. You probably know better than me."

Katie blushed and her green eyes glistened. Cord was taken by surprise. She had the appearance of a woman who could handle almost any situation. Maybe it was the determined look in her eyes or the way she carried herself. He used to watch John Wayne movies with his dad. Katie reminded him of the actress Maureen O'Hara, the redheaded heroine who was often in those movies. Maureen O'Hara had never backed down, or at least he didn't remember her backing down.

"Gwen, this is your wedding."

"And you're my sister. I have my residency and I know this is bad timing…"

"But I can't stay here without you and expcct everyone to haul me around."

"I need you here," Gwen continued. Next to her, Dr. Jeff looked at his watch. Cord glanced from the doctor to Katie and saw a woman who was probably used to caving in when it came to her sister.

"I'd be honored to give you a lift over to the ranch, Miss Archer." He nearly groaned as the words slipped out. Thinking she looked like the redheaded Irish actress Maureen O'Hara didn't mean he had to start talking and acting like John Wayne.

He was thirty-four and the last thing he needed was to get caught in this family drama. He especially didn't like the look on Julie's face as she headed his way. Now that she'd fallen in love, she seemed to want everyone to have a happy ending. Cord's happy ending included him sitting by his lake with a fishing pole, his best dog and a thermos of coffee. Like their dad, Julie would have to realize that everyone was fair game in the matchmaking business but him.

"Really, I don't see…" Katie tried to reject his offer. Julie was steps away from making contact with them.

Gwen's hand was on her arm. "I'll be back by the end of next week. I know I'm leaving sooner than we expected, but please, can you stay for me?"

"You know I'll do it, Gwen."

"Maybe you can help out with some of the other plans." Gwen looped an arm through her sister's and smiled up at her. "You'll be bored and that will give you something to do while I'm gone."

He could have sworn Katie mumbled something about not having her own life, but she smiled and told her sister of course she would help.

And then Julie was at his side, smiling her bright smile. "With your fashion background maybe you can help with the dresses!"

"The brides aren't supplying their own dresses?" Katie looked at him for the answer, not Julie.

"We have a few companies willing to loan vintage dresses for the women who don't have a vintage dress of their own. Wedding apparel is a little out of my comfort zone."

"I thought you had a wedding coordinator?" Katie was now interested.

"We do have a wedding coordinator—Helen Avery—but she's had a difficult time showing up. When I do see her, I want to know what we need so that we don't have to just rely on her for the arrangements."

"I see." Katie glanced at her sister, a fresh wave of pain settling in those green eyes of hers. She flashed another smile, though. "I think my sister plans on wearing our great-grandmother's dress. I believe you want the dresses to be from the early twentieth century, between 1900 and 1920."

"I think so," Cord hedged, glanced at his watch and started to think of excuses for escaping.

As much as he wanted to escape, Katie seemed just as in need. Her sister was talking, discussing the dress with seed pearls, handmade lace from Bavaria and silk so soft it might possibly fall apart if washed.

"I never wanted the dress," Gwen Archer smiled at him and then reached for her fiancé's hand. "But then this wedding came up and we both want this. We want to be married here, in a ceremony that means something to this community."

He shook his head and bit back the reply that

almost slipped out. Special? A ceremony with forty-nine other couples. He wouldn't exactly put that under the heading of special, sentimental or anything else with meaning. It was his dad's idea. It was another way to put Jasper Gulch on the map. If Cord had his way, he'd call the whole thing off, tell these couples to go home and plan a sweet ceremony in their local church with people they care about in attendance rather than eight guests per couple and half the town of Jasper Gulch.

But none of that mattered because Katie lifted her hand to flick away a tear that rolled down her cheek. All while her sister continued to talk about that dress she hadn't really wanted to wear.

Okay, he was a rescuer by nature. He'd hoped to keep that part of himself tamped down, locked up and out of sight. But the glisten of tears in Katie's eyes, the way she managed to smile and agree with her sister about how perfect this would be, couldn't be ignored.

"Let me give you a ride to the ranch, Miss Archer. I'm about done in with wedding planning and I'd imagine you've had a long day."

"I have had a long day," she agreed and her gaze met his, silently thanking him. For the first time in a long time he was happy to be a rescuer.

Gwen shot her a look and then stepped closer

to Dr. Jeff. "Then I guess we'll head back to Missoula. Are you sure you'll be okay here, Katie?"

Katie smiled, nodded and told her sister she'd be just fine and she'd make notes about the ceremony. And Gwen needed to make sure she got the dress fitted. It would be long for her and probably too big around the waist.

Gwen hugged her sister. "I know you always wanted to wear it, Katie. But it will be perfect for this ceremony and I'll make sure they take it up but don't cut it. We can always let it out for you when you get married."

Katie smiled. "Of course we can."

Cord offered Katie his arm, knowing he'd regret it, knowing there were plenty of people watching who would talk later, make up stories and have him married off to the redhead from Missoula. He shook off regret and waited, looking down at her as she made the decision to take his arm. He gave her an encouraging smile. She nodded and her hand settled on his sleeve.

"Thank you, Mr. Shaw."

"Cord."

She nodded and looked away. "Then you should call me Katie."

He led her out of the festival hall into the dark night and a sky twinkling with millions of stars. The air was cold now that the sun had gone down. "You don't have a coat in there, do you?"

"No, it seemed warm earlier and I left my coat and suitcase at your parents' house."

He held up a remote start. "My truck should be warm."

Next to him she nodded but he saw her shiver. He slipped out of his jacket and placed it over her shoulders. She smiled up at him and he thought she had about the prettiest smile he'd ever seen. But he drew back from that thought like a man twice bitten by a poisonous snake.

Twice bitten, twice engaged and jilted, all the same thing to Cord Shaw and he wasn't going there again. But he could be a gentleman, a cowboy, and give Katie a ride home. He'd even walk her to the front door, make sure she got inside safely, and then he'd head on back to his little cabin on the banks of Shaw Lake.

He opened the truck door and she climbed in, handing him back his jacket. "Don't worry, Mr. Shaw, I'm not on the hunt. I'm here for my sister, not to follow in her footsteps but to be here to support her."

"I hadn't thought—"

She smiled, cutting off his explanations. "No, you hadn't. But everyone else will think it. A relationship and marriage are the last thing I want."

Interesting. He would have questioned her more, but he thought asking questions might push them a little too far into each other's lives. She'd given him enough of an explanation and he was willing to let her leave it at that.

True to his best intentions, he drove her to the Shaw ranch, walked her to the front door of the house he'd been raised in, saw her safely inside and told her he was sure they'd see each other the next day.

It was that easy.

Or at least he had thought it would be easy. But driving away from the ranch after dropping her off, he realized her scent lingered in his truck. He lifted his jacket to his nose and sniffed. Yeah, that was her. The scent was oriental, not sweet and flowery.

He grinned and draped the jacket over the seat as he headed down the bumpy trail toward his place. All the while her scent teased him and he thought that it might be nice to spend time with a woman who spoke her mind. It would be easy. And in a month she'd be gone. That made her just about perfect.

Chapter Two

Katie walked downstairs Sunday morning, her second day in the Shaw home and her second day feeling out of place. She didn't belong here, not in this town or in this house. This was Gwen's moment, not Katie's. And yet, here she was.

She took a deep breath and put on a smile and hopefully a look of confidence. She could do this. Following the sound of laughter and voices raised in numerous conversations, she walked through the pine-paneled living room and headed toward the big country kitchen with its long, butcher-block table, gleaming granite countertops and light oak cabinets. Julie Shaw, auburn hair and blue eyes, turned to smile at her.

"Good morning, Katie. Do you want coffee? And we have muffins, bacon and sausage this morning. Breakfast is simple on Sundays." Julie's long, auburn hair curled down past her shoulders.

She wore her typical homespun sweater but today with a skirt.

"Coffee and a muffin sounds great," Katie admitted.

Julie pointed to a plate and clean cups. Katie had been told that Julie Shaw raised sheep for their wool. She had an internet business selling that wool and hand-knit items she made. Katie loved fashion and could appreciate the beauty of Julie's creations. Before she left town, she planned on buying several items.

"There's fresh coffee in the pot," Julie continued. "But you have to hurry. It's the second pot we've made and with this many people in the house it won't last long."

Julie lived in her own house on the Shaw property. Katie had seen the little place from a distance and the field dotted with the sheep Julie raised for their wool.

"Thank you." Katie looked around the kitchen, smiling at Nadine Shaw and her daughter Faith Shaw, who had just walked through the door. Both were dressed for church.

Faith wasn't the youngest Shaw, but she was the tiniest. She and Julie shared the auburn hair they had probably inherited from their mother, and the blue eyes of their father. But Faith was tiny and less inclined to gab at the drop of a hat. Julie had told Katie that Faith played the violin for the Bozeman Symphony, but she'd gone to Seattle for a short time. It hadn't worked out was the only answer given when asked why Faith hadn't stayed.

"Do you attend church, Katie?" Faith asked as she poured herself a cup of coffee. She was dressed in a cute denim-and-lace dress, turquoise-and-brown cowboy boots and a scarf around her neck.

Katie looked over the top of her cup. Did she attend church? She hadn't been raised in church, but last year a friend, seeing that Katie was a train wreck about to happen, had shared faith with her and invited her to spend a few weekends in the small town where she lived so that Katie could attend church. She'd gone and she'd found something that filled a huge void in her life that she'd been trying to fill with relationships. Going-nowhere relationships.

"I'd love to go to church," she finally answered. "If that's okay."

"Of course it is," Julie gave her a careful look. "Do you go to church in Missoula?"

Katie shook her head. "Not usually. I just haven't known where to go."

Or how to walk in alone. She definitely wouldn't have the alone problem today, not with this group of people.

Faith walked up behind her, giving her a tight hug and taking her by surprise. "You'll love our little mountain church. Well, it isn't little. I guess it must have been at one time, but it's been built on to."

"Is everyone about ready to head for church? Those who are going?" Jackson Shaw walked into the kitchen, taking up more space than a man should. His very presence commanded respect, Katie thought. And he made her shake in her shoes, just a little.

"Katie's going," Julie offered. "And I think Michael and Helen. Oh, and Thomas and Mandy plus her sister, Beth."

She pointed to one of the couples that would be getting married at the end of the month. Another couple entered the room, along with the sister of the bride. Beth. Katie had met Beth the previous evening. She was a pretty brunette, petite with big brown eyes. Katie felt like a giant in comparison.

"No need taking half a dozen cars." Jackson looked around the room, his lips moving as he counted. "We'll take the Suburban and if Cord shows up, someone can ride with him."

"Cord doesn't usually go to church," Julie shared in a whisper for Katie only.

Cord didn't attend church? That piece of the puzzle didn't fit. It was like putting a corner piece in the middle and trying to make it work. He was a Shaw from Jasper Gulch. It seemed to her that church and faith would be part of his DNA.

Before she could comment, there were footsteps and Cord's voice coming from the direction of the living room. His voice was low and husky as he spoke to someone. The dog, his mother's poodle, barked. He told the dog to be quiet. When he entered the room, carrying the poodle and talking to his mom, Katie had a moment. She told herself it wasn't one of *those* moments, the kind when you see a guy and something amazing happens. It was a moment that was sweet and undefined but precious. Cord Shaw seemed like a good, decent man.

He was also a man in his mid-thirties who had never married. There had to be a reason for that.

Twice bitten kept coming back to her. Who had said that about Cord Shaw? Did that mean he'd been married twice, or rejected twice?

It didn't matter. Her attention drifted to take in his appearance, even though she said she didn't care. If his father filled up space, Cord Shaw took the oxygen. He was dressed in jeans, boots and a button-down shirt. But no hat. His dark wavy hair caught her attention because it looked as if he'd brushed it with his fingers. As if he'd read her mind, he brushed a hand across the top of his head, pushing the wayward strands into some type of order.

"Why's everyone looking at me?" Cord glanced around. On second look she realized he wasn't dressed for church. His jeans were faded, his shirt was flannel and his boots were worn.

He glanced at his dad and neither of them smiled.

Family dynamics and more of the tension she'd felt the previous evening.

"We're filling up the Suburban to go to church and I think we have too many people." As Jackson spoke, Cord started backing up. Jackson glanced around the crowd and without saying anything, his sharp gaze landed on the very pretty Beth. Then his gaze shifted to Katie.

Cord followed his dad's look and he shook his head. "I wasn't going to church."

"Well, it sure would make things easier if you would." Jackson didn't bother hinting.

Cord didn't look like a man who cared what anyone thought or expected from him. As the family scattered, grabbing jackets and purses, Katie turned to follow.

"Fine, I'll go. Katie, looks like you're riding with me."

She turned, her mouth open. And what was she supposed to say to something that hadn't been a question and didn't even sound as if it was what the man wanted? She got it, she was the easiest choice. Beth had that look, the kind that said she was searching for romance, for her own walk down the aisle. Katie was used to the role of friend.

"Excuse me?" she blurted out, shifting her purse over her shoulder.

"Beth would probably prefer to ride with her sister," Cord said with a shrug that said he'd made a logical choice.

"Yes, of course." Katie looked around the room seeking an ally. Everyone seemed to be content with the plan. Everyone but Beth, who cast a jealous look at her as she left with her sister. Julie, whom Katie thought might be a friend, just smiled and hurried out of the room.

"I'm really sorry," Katie offered as she walked out the front door with Cord.

He smiled at her. "Katie, if you want to go to church, you should go. And if I have to go, I prefer taking someone I can at least have a conversation with."

"Thank you." She didn't know if it was the correct response, but what else could she say? Once again she'd been put in a box, the one labeled Friend. She told herself she was good with that. After all, she'd been a new-and-improved Katie for the past year. No more chasing after love. No more insecurity. Friend was safe. She wanted safe.

Cord had to count to ten as he walked around the front of his truck to the driver's-side door.

He didn't know exactly how his perfect fishing day had turned into a date, or was it church, with Katie? But here he was climbing in his truck and heading for the main road and church. With Katie at his side.

Once again his dad was the one to thank.

In the seat next to him, Katie toyed with her purse, fiddled with the necklace hanging around her neck and then watched out the window as the scenery passed them by. Did she see what he saw? That it was a perfect morning for fishing? The air was brisk and smelled of drying leaves and pine. There were a few white clouds chasing each other across a perfect azure sky. They wouldn't have many more mornings like this.

Well, maybe God would appreciate his sacrifice and bless him with some decent trout. Not that God worked that way. He wasn't so far gone that he didn't still believe, still pray, still take time for the Almighty. He just had a few issues to work out.

"I'm sorry," Katie finally said. Her voice was clear, bright, sweet.

Strong.

He had the overwhelming impression of strength when he looked at Katie. But there was more to her than that, there was something in her expression, something a little lost about her.

"Why are you sorry?" He glanced her way and then refocused on the road.

"That you've been stuck with me again."

"I'm sorry if I made you feel that way. I'm going to be honest with you, I'd feel stuck no matter who they put in my truck. I think my dad put me in charge of this wedding thinking it would make me all romantic, give me ideas about forever and the like."

"And?" She smiled a big smile and those green eyes twinkled. For the first time since he walked into the main ranch, he felt a little easier on the inside.

"It makes me want to run as fast as I can in the other direction. Your sister and her fiancé seem decent but I've heard more bickering and arguing in the past week, since the couples for the wedding arrived in town. There is a couple staying with a family in town. She knows this wedding is vintage but she's got this dress ordered from New York, and why can't she have her own cake, and what about her aunt Milly from Oregon?"

"I think I met that bride last night. Andrea, I think. You're safe with me, though. We can be birds of a feather."

Smiling came a little easier. "I'm glad to hear that. So, you think they were going to toss Beth my way?"

"She's pretty and very sweet. They're going to throw the most tempting package at you."

"And you think you're not…" Well, now, how in the world did he continue this conversation and not sound like a jerk or the world's biggest flirt?

"Tempting?"

"You think Beth is more tempting?" He cleared his throat, feeling pretty uncomfortable with this whole conversation. But she was laughing now and he enjoyed her laughter. When he looked at her, she shrugged in answer to his question.

If he was going to have to go to church, he might as well have a good time. He wouldn't have enjoyed it with Beth at his side. He'd met her two days ago and she'd made pretty big hints. No, not hints. She'd outright asked him to show her the town. The next day she'd told him she'd heard about the café and the homemade pies but she was stuck with her sister.

His phone buzzed and he gave her an apologetic look and answered because it was finally the wedding planner. "Cord Shaw."

He listened. He tried to argue. He counted to ten, more than once. And then he tossed his phone on the seat.

"Bad news."

"Yeah."

"They put your name down with Beth's as the fiftieth couple?"

He smiled and he hadn't meant to smile. "No. That was the wedding coordinator. She's quitting. She was doing this pretty much free and she got a better offer, one that pays."

"Ouch. So now what?"

"I'm not sure."

He pulled into the parking lot of the church that his family had been attending for generations and that he'd been avoiding as much as possible for a few years. Avoiding because he and God hadn't seen eye to eye on several things. A broken engagement when he was twenty. And then at twenty-nine a fiancée who ran off with his best man two weeks before they were to get married in this very church. Those were his reasons for avoiding relationships. His reason for avoiding God had more to do with Marci. He shoved the thought away because he couldn't go there right now, not with Katie sitting in his truck waiting to go to church. The look on her face was something close to a kid's on Christmas morning.

He shook his head, amused in spite of himself. He hadn't expected to go to church when he woke up that morning. He really hadn't expected to be there with a woman he barely knew getting out of the passenger side of his truck. But there he was, standing on the sidewalk, the rustic church with wood siding, stone and stained glass behind him.

The sign out front with the name Mountainview Church of the Savior also had smaller print telling the history behind the church. Most folks just called it Mountainview now, and everyone knew which church they meant.

"With no coordinator to help, will you call off the wedding?" Katie asked as she stepped next to him.

"No." He couldn't explain to her that there was too much at stake. The town needed this wedding and the money it would bring in. They had a bridge in need of repairs and a museum they couldn't finish without more funds. "I'll just figure out how to pull off a wedding for fifty couples, maybe get some media attention for Jasper Gulch and hopefully not mess up anyone's life."

"I think you'll do just fine. Remember, it's all about the dress."

"How long are you going to be in town, Katie?" He placed a hand on her back and guided her up the sidewalk that had a few uneven places.

"I'm not sure. I'm supposed to be helping my sister, but she seems to have escaped and left me here." She sighed and glanced at him. "I'm sorry, that wasn't fair. Gwen is in a residency program and of course her time off is limited. And Jeff has a practice to tend to. I have several weeks of vacation and several personal days that I planned on taking so I could be here to help Gwen."

"Do you always give up your time to help your sister?"

She looked away and he was sorry he had asked. Especially when she smiled at him a moment later, a hint of sadness in her eyes. "She would do the same for me."

"Of course. I didn't mean…" What had he meant? "It's really none of my business."

"You don't have to apologize. I'm okay with being here, and with helping her."

"Do you think that as long as you're here…"

He didn't know what to say. They were standing in front of the massive wooden doors that led to the church. She had a slightly red nose from the cool morning air and her lips were tinted with pink gloss. As long as she was there, she could be a friend. That wasn't what he'd planned to say but the thought framed itself as a question in his mind.

She was studying his face, waiting for him to finish.

"Maybe you could help me with this wedding?" He asked the question that had originally been on his mind.

"Me?"

"You obviously have more fashion sense than I do. For me, dressed up is a sport jacket with my jeans and a pair of boots that I only wear to town or for special occasions."

"I see. I thought maybe you wanted me to run interference and keep the single women at bay. Hands off Cord Shaw, that kind of thing." As she said it, somehow her palm came to rest on his shoulder as if they'd been friends forever.

It was the strangest and maybe one of the best feelings. It tangled him up and made him lose track of the reality that he was standing in front of church. People he'd known his whole life were walking their way. The door could open at any moment. And for the first time in years a woman had made him feel at ease.

"That wasn't what I was thinking," he finally said. "But your plan does have merit."

"Of course it does." Her hand slipped away and she took a step back.

"So, you'll help me?"

"Keep the women at bay?"

"With the wedding?"

"I'm not sure I want to be that involved." Her voice was soft. "I already have to be my sister's right-hand woman. I'm not sure I can be that and help you."

"I would be forever in your debt."

"The times I've heard..." She smiled and didn't finish. "I'll think about it. But I think you probably need someone local who has more knowledge of the area and what's available. I've been a bridesmaid a few times. That is my total experience with weddings."

"I've never made it down the aisle, so you have more experience than me." He pushed the double doors open and then with a hand on her arm he guided her down the aisle to the pew behind his family.

He glanced behind them, looking for Marci and her grandmother. He'd promised to take Marci riding after church. No matter how busy he was during the week, he always managed to spend time with her on Sunday. It was their day. It was his way of keeping a promise to a friend.

He hadn't been to church too often since the day of Marci's mother's funeral.

And yet, here he was, sitting next to Katie Archer, trying not to weep over the loss of a friend, a girl without a mother, and soon…

He couldn't think about soon, or about what Lulu Jenson, Marci's grandmother, was going to face in the near future. In the seat next to him, Katie moved, turning to look around the old building. He tried to see it through her eyes, with the golden glass of the windows, the polished wooden pews, the history.

At the back of the church and on the opposite side he saw Marci with Lulu. The two waved and he smiled. Both of them looked a little too happy to see him there. In the pew in front of him his mother turned to smile, the look in her eyes saying she thought a prayer had been answered. He was back in church. It had been a while.

He settled back in his seat and ignored the woman next to him and the questioning look she gave him. Because she was the one person he didn't really have to worry about answering to. She'd be gone in a month. Their stories weren't connected.

But he couldn't ignore her, not completely. Not when he caught a scent of the oriental perfume that had followed him into his house last night, clinging to the jacket he'd slipped over her shoulders.

She was temporary in this town, and in his life. What was permanent for Cord Shaw were the people in this church. The people connected to him each and every day, counting on him to be there for them.

Right now it felt as if there were a lot of people needing him to pull off this Old Tyme Wedding. There were fifty couples counting on the wedding of the century at the end of the month. Jasper Gulch was counting on him. They needed this wedding. They needed it to bring in funds. They needed it to keep them all united.

He needed a wedding coordinator. The woman next to him moved, her arm brushing his. He didn't glance her way because he wasn't going to be obvious, but it was obvious to him that she might be the best person for the job. He knew she worked in fashion. She knew what it would take to put this event together. And bonus, she didn't appear to be a woman on the hunt for a groom of her own.

Chapter Three

The church service ended with a prayer and a closing song. Katie sat for a moment, reflecting on the words of the sermon, a sermon about faith and persevering in troubled times. She couldn't say that she'd ever really had troubled times. Her life hadn't been perfect, but she'd never gone without or faced real tragedies.

Next to her, Cord moved and stood. She wondered if he would leave now and continue with the fishing trip he had planned. Before she could ask, a lightning streak of a girl zoomed down the aisle of the church and grabbed his hand. She appeared to be a preteen, perhaps ten or eleven years of age. Her blond hair was braided and she wore jeans and a sweater. With a look she dismissed Katie.

"Cord, you're at church!"

"Yes, I am. Don't act so surprised."

She laughed and held on to his hand, at the same time shooting Katie a curious look. "But you never come to church. I thought you would pick me up at Grammy's."

A daughter? Katie watched, wondering but knowing it had nothing to do with her. She stood and glanced around, looking for Julie, because with Cord's younger sister she felt as if she had a friend in the strange world she'd been left in. She would thank Gwen for that. For making her feel like a pet left on the side of the road.

Cord was speaking to the girl and Katie overheard part of the conversation. "Since I'm here I don't have to pick you up at your grammy's."

"Who is she?" the young girl asked.

"She's Katie and she's staying with my parents. Don't be rude."

Miss Preteen stared Katie down, curious and territorial. "Are you getting married?"

"No, my sister is," Katie answered.

"Then shouldn't she be here?"

Katie smiled at that, liking the girl even if she asked a lot of questions. "She should, but she had to go to work. Now, you know a lot about me, why don't you tell me your name."

"Marci." Marci had big brown eyes and nothing about her features, her hair or eyes, resembled Cord Shaw.

"I see. And are you going fishing with Cord?"

Marci shook her head. “No, he was supposed to go fishing and then take me riding.”

Katie couldn’t help that she wanted to know who the girl was to Cord. But neither Marci nor Cord seemed to be giving up details.

“That sounds like fun,” was all she could think to say. She glanced around, still looking for Julie. She saw her finally, holding the hand of her fiancé, Ryan, and chatting with a group of people similar in age. She knew from Julie’s sister, Faith, that Ryan Travers had come to town for the rodeo and stayed. The reason for his putting down roots in Jasper Gulch was pretty obvious as he smiled at the young woman holding his arm. Katie looked away, uncomfortable with that easy gesture between Julie and Ryan.

The sun shone through the golden stained-glass windows of the church, catching everything in the warm light. Katie forgot the crowd of people. She forgot the turmoil of the past few days. She allowed Cord to step away with the girl, Marci, the two deep in conversation that had nothing to do with her.

The golden light, the soft scent of wood polish and the hum of conversations, it all melded together and Katie felt the peace she’d been looking for. When she went home to Missoula, she would find a church like this one.

Or maybe she would never leave Jasper Gulch.

The thought took her by surprise. It was a silly idea, one that came out of nowhere and made no sense. She couldn't stay here. She didn't have a job, probably couldn't find a job and she didn't have family in the area. What would she do in Jasper Gulch?

"Katie, there you are." Julie appeared in front of her and Katie managed a smile, shaking free from random thoughts of moving, leaving behind the life she had in Missoula.

"Here I am," she responded with a smile.

"We're all going to town for lunch. Do you want to join us?"

Katie looked around, searching for Cord. He'd walked off and was a short distance away, Marci next to him. The older woman he was speaking to had to be Marci's grandmother. As the two adults talked, Marci shifted from foot to foot. The girl turned, caught Katie's gaze on her and smiled. Katie returned the gesture but then focused on Julie's question about lunch. Cord had moved on with his own plans. She could move on with hers. Not that she really had plans.

"Lunch would be good," she told Julie. "Where will we go?"

"The diner in town has a Sunday special. Usually something yummy like pot roast or fried chicken." Julie looked from Katie to Cord and back to Katie. Her eyes twinkled with mischief. "Unless you have other plans."

"No, of course not. I was just thinking that I probably need to find another ride to the Shaw ranch. Cord seems to have plans and I don't want him to feel like he has to give me a ride."

Julie nodded in agreement. "He usually does something with Marci on Sundays. It's their day together."

"I see." But she didn't see. "Is her mother here?"

Julie's smile dissolved and she shook her head. "No, Marci's mom died when she was a baby. Her grandmother, Lulu Jenson, has raised her."

The story settled in Katie's heart and she felt a wave of pain she hadn't expected. She shouldn't have asked, but now that she knew Marci's story it mattered. It made sense of a man she barely knew, made him more real, more like someone a woman would want to spend time with.

"I'm sorry, I shouldn't have asked."

"It isn't as if it's a secret. Cord would have told you, if he'd had a moment to spare."

Katie didn't agree, but she didn't say that to Julie. To Cord Shaw, Katie was practically a stranger. He didn't owe her stories about his life or about a child that seemed a very big part of his life.

"She's cute and she obviously loves your brother."

At that Julie laughed. "She does love him and

he does spoil her rotten. Sometimes I think he uses her as an excuse, though."

Katie pretended not to hear the last comment made by a sister about her older brother. What Cord did in his personal life was really none of her business. For that reason she changed the subject. "Are you sure you have room for me?"

Julie slipped an arm through Katie's. "Of course we do. There are plenty of us Shaws here at church, so we'll have more room heading over to the diner. I'm riding with Ryan and you can go with us."

"That sounds great. I'll just let Cord know so he doesn't wonder where I've gone to."

Julie pointed and Katie turned to find Cord standing behind her. Somehow she got lost for a minute in the blue of his eyes and in the smile that shifted the rugged planes of his face, emphasizing the scar near his eye and the dimple in his left cheek. A shaft of sunlight filtered through the windows, catching the slightest bit of gray at his temples. And then the sunlight was gone and the room seemed darker.

Words evaded her and she really needed to say something. Anything to put this moment to rest. And suddenly Marci was at her side, giving her the break she needed.

"Do you like to ride?" Marci asked, in maybe not the friendliest tone.

"I'm sorry?"

Katie heard Julie excuse herself and before she could stop the other woman, she was gone. Katie started to call out to her because she was an ally of sorts. Marci's hand reached for hers, drawing her attention back to the man and girl standing in front of her.

"I'm sorry, ride?" Katie looked from Marci to Cord.

"Horses," Marci said with a preteen roll of the eyes.

"Oh, horses."

"Yes, horses." Cord was smiling now.

She didn't know if she liked to ride horses, but she knew she wanted to. She would be in Jasper Gulch for most of the month and she wanted to enjoy herself. And she could enjoy herself with Cord Shaw and Marci. No entanglements. No temptations.

He was a man who wanted only friendship. And maybe help planning this monstrosity of a wedding.

The last thing Cord had planned to do was bring Katie Archer into this part of his life. He protected Marci and Lulu. That had been his job for almost as long as Marci had been alive. But Marci had other ideas this time. For some reason she was clinging to Katie's hand, pleading with her to go riding.

He wanted to smile at the trapped look on her face. Her jewel-colored eyes were flitting from his goddaughter to him and back to Marci. It would have made his life easier if she'd met Marci and quickly slipped away, uninterested in this part of his life. Instead, she seemed to be silently asking his permission.

Great.

He'd gone several years without getting tangled up or inviting a woman into this part of his life. He'd learned his lesson with his ex-fiancée, Susan. She'd told him from the beginning that she didn't want Marci in their lives. He hadn't realized until it was too late that she'd been serious. It had all become crystal clear when she'd thrown him over for his best man—his supposed best friend.

Lesson learned.

"Marci told me she wouldn't mind if you joined us," he admitted now to Katie because she was still standing there looking unsure. She seemed to be waiting for permission to accept. Great.

"We really don't mind," he continued.

And he'd love to see her on a horse, the city girl in her made-for-dresses riding boots, the scarf around her neck and hair falling in loose curls.

"I see." She bit down on her bottom lip and then looked around.

"They all assumed you'd go and they've left you behind," he explained the obvious. The church had emptied out.

"We have a picnic," Marci offered with a hesitant smile. "And Cord has a real gentle horse."

"Does he?" Katie looked down, smiling at his goddaughter.

He felt a real fondness for this woman, practically a stranger, at that moment. Her hesitation wasn't about Marci. Maybe it was more that she just wasn't interested in him. Or was she afraid of horses?

"Do you ride?" he asked.

"I've been once, on a trail horse."

"The nose-to-tail kind of trail horse?" he asked, unable to hold back his amusement.

"Yes, that's the kind."

"Don't worry, you'll be fine."

Pastor Ethan Johnson approached, ending the conversation. Cord smiled at the other man because he and Ethan had something in common. They were both on the list of eligible bachelors in Jasper Gulch. Men who needed to find wives. He, for one, didn't need help. Ethan probably felt the same way.

There were plenty of single ladies in town. There were even a few new ones. There were the

Shoemaker ladies, the new historian from somewhere in New Mexico, Cord's sister Faith. The list was long. Cord knew his dad would like to see all of his kids married off. More than once lately Jackson and Nadine Shaw had mentioned that it was high time someone put some grandkids in those empty bedrooms at the ranch.

"Are you all heading out?" Pastor Ethan asked as he walked up to them, smiling at Marci and then at Katie.

Katie gave Ethan a friendly smile but not the flirty one so many single woman used on the pastor. She was definitely one of a kind. He liked that about her.

"Yes, we are and we're sorry for keeping you late, Ethan. I didn't realize everyone had left." Cord glanced around the empty church. The church he'd been raised in.

It hadn't changed much over the years. The wooden pews, the amber glass in the windows, all exactly as it had been the last time he'd come to church. It felt the same, smelled the same. The only thing that had changed was him.

"Haven't seen you here before, have I, Cord?"

Cord smiled at that. Ethan had never seen him here. "No, I guess I haven't been here since you took over."

"No, I guess not." Ethan shot a quick look at Katie and then back to Cord. "Things change."

Not that way, they didn't. He wouldn't hurt Katie's feelings by opposing the statement too heavily and what it implied.

"I reckon they do." Cord touched Marci's back to guide her toward the door. "And we should get out of here so you can lock up."

Ethan walked to the front of the church with them. "Cord, I heard that with the siding on the museum, they might get some finish work done on the interior by the end of the month."

"If we don't run out of money."

"I've found some photographs of the church that I thought might be something for the historical society, as well as an older Bible that has been left in the office. It should really be put under glass. There are even some births and family histories included."

"Sounds like something we'd love to have in the museum, Ethan. You might even show it to Robin Frazier, she's in town studying genealogy, I believe."

"I think I've seen her."

They were at the doors now and Cord watched as Marci, who had hurried out ahead of them, tried to get the truck door open. He hit the remote to unlock it and she shot him a big smile and climbed inside.

"She's got more energy than ten kids," Ethan said. He glanced up and then back at Cord. "It's a shame to have that bell up there and no way to use it."

"Yeah, I don't guess I remember that bell ever working," Cord said.

"You know, if they insist on using the recorded bells instead of fixing this one, we could always remove the bell and put it in the museum," Ethan said, looking up at the door in the ceiling that led to the belfry.

"I could bring it up with the church council. To be honest, I don't even know what's wrong with the bell."

"Neither do I. When I got here I was told there's a bell but it doesn't work and they showed me how to use the recordings." As Ethan talked, he reached to undo the collar around his neck. "If you could bring up the issue, I'd appreciate it."

"I'll do it."

The two men shook hands and then Cord turned to ask Katie if she was ready to go. Katie had already walked away. She was at the truck with Marci and he could tell from the distance that the two of them were having an animated conversation. He said a final goodbye to Ethan and headed down the sidewalk to see what was waiting for him.

On the way to his place, Cord decided to quiz Katie to find out what he could about weddings. He'd always been an organizer, but he was finding that weddings were way out of his realm of expertise. He knew computers. He could develop software. He helped market his sister's wool. But weddings were not his thing. *Really* not his thing. He'd had two brides and not managed to get either of them down the aisle.

"What exactly is the plan for the wedding?" Katie asked, her smile saying what he already knew, that this wedding was just about ridiculous.

"It's a long process, that's the plan." He reached to turn down the radio and pushed Marci's hand away when she went for the volume. "I think the plan for this wedding is to drive me crazy."

"That bad?"

"That bad." He slowed the truck to ease through the open gate that led to his place. "When my dad plans something, he plans big. It's why he wanted me to run for city council, so he would have help with this big centennial celebration. We couldn't do just a weekend in the summer. Even the week I suggested wasn't good enough. No, Jackson Shaw wants something that people will talk about, something that will draw people to town and hopefully give us a jump-start on reclaiming the Jasper Gulch of yesteryear."

Not everyone had been on board. There were people in town who didn't welcome new business or all of the traffic the centennial celebration had brought.

Or the drama. The missing time capsule started the whole thing off with a bang. Then came vandalism at the rodeo and the fire at the fairgrounds the previous month. At least his dad had gotten something out of that picnic. He'd gotten Faith hooked up with Pastor Ethan for a single day. Cord didn't think his sister had seen the pastor since.

Cord figured there had to be another way to jump-start the town he'd grown up in. An easier way than staging a wedding with fifty couples. Especially if he was going to have to be the guy in charge.

He glanced at Katie. "The way things have been going, something crazy is sure to happen at this wedding. Are you positive you don't want to be the new coordinator?"

"I think I'm pretty sure I don't want the job. If I can help…"

The offer, made with some hesitation, took him by surprise. Cord pulled up to his little log house at the edge of Shaw Lake. It wasn't a big lake, just five acres of fresh water from an underground spring and runoff from melting snow.

"I know we have dresses we can borrow and a business that will make flower arrangements, a bakery for the cakes and a caterer for the reception." He'd been making plans for months, with the wedding coordinator handling details and giving him information.

"So you're down to the final details?"

He opened his truck door but didn't get out. "Yes, final preparations. The bouquets have to be ordered. I think there is an assortment of fall colors the women can choose from. The dress choices have to be finalized and fitted by a local seamstress. And of course we have a committee to decorate the tents the day of the wedding."

"You should probably have the brides finish picking their dresses. Some of the fittings might take time. Especially if the women aren't in town."

"That's the kind of help I'm talking about." He only wished he could talk her into taking over. But he also knew the rumors that would start if she did, and if they were seen spending too much time together. Not that he cared too much about talk. He'd been creating talk most of his adult life.

Marci sighed and gave him a pointed look. "Do you think you two wedding planners could work on this later?"

Cord laughed at his goddaughter and pushed his door open. She was already climbing out the backdoor of his truck. "I think we can get this show on the road."

As they walked up to his house, Katie stopped

to look around. She stood in his wild, overgrown mess of a yard, all wildflowers and shrubs. He could have put down sod for grass, but he liked the wild look. The house was a two-story, log with plenty of windows facing south and west to catch the heat of the sun and to give the best view of the lake. A short distance from the house were his private stables, a barn and the acreage where he kept his horses.

He raised some of the best quarter horses in the state. It wasn't that the Shaw family didn't have quality horses and love their animals, but Cord took his horses a little more seriously. He raised cutting horses and sold them all over the country. His best stallion had sired several champions and had been a champion himself.

"This is beautiful," Katie turned once more and looked back at him. "And secluded. Being out here could make a person feel like they were alone in the world."

"Yeah, sometimes," he admitted. But it never really bothered him. Being duped, being let down by someone you trust, those were the things that bothered Cord.

"Hello, hungry kid here." Marci reentered the conversation with those words.

Cord growled and chased her up the front steps of the house. "Marci, you're getting worse every day."

"Grammy says it's your fault I'm spoiled."

"Yeah, I think she has to take some of the credit."

He opened the door of the house and ushered Marci in and then held the door for Katie. It took her a few minutes. She stood at the foot of the stone steps looking around, turning in slow circles. He tried to see the area through her eyes. The wide stretching valley, grasslands that were often sprinkled with wildflowers. In the distance cattle grazed. He could barely make out the smoke from the fireplace at the main ranch.

It had been a long time since he'd brought anyone other than family to this house. As he followed Katie inside a few minutes later, he glanced around the adequately sized living room with the braided rugs, deep red leather furniture and stone fireplace. It was a good place to live. The only feminine touches came from gifts his sisters or mother gave at Christmas or on birthdays. And there were throw pillows. He had a weird feeling his sister Julie sneaked in from time to time just to add little things. A throw pillow here, a bouquet of flowers there, sometimes flowery-smelling hand soap. All the things she knew would drive him crazy.

He'd started thinking he might put a wildlife camera outside. Just to catch her in the act. He thought it would be fun to watch her creeping in with whatever feminine assault she planned.

The house had three bedrooms upstairs. He had an office and a family room at the back of the house on the main floor. More than enough room for a bachelor who spent most of his time outside. Katie followed Marci to the kitchen. He'd gotten sidetracked and the two of them were ahead of him, laughing about something. He watched Katie lean down to hear something Marci said. The moment caught him by surprise.

It was good for Marci to have these moments. Life would change soon enough. There was nothing he could do about what would happen in the coming days, weeks or months. He shoved away the troubling thoughts and smiled at Marci, the girl who was going to need him more than anyone ever had.

That thought was enough to put him back on track and keep him focused on what was important in his life.

"Is there something I can do?" Katie stood in his kitchen, red hair that framed her pretty face and green eyes that were studying him, as he moved toward the fridge.

"I'm going to put some sandwiches in a pack, maybe some chips, cookies and bottled water. It shouldn't take long to get it all together." Okay, the truth was that Sandy Wilson, his parents' housekeeper and right-hand woman, had already made the sandwiches. Four of them, bagged and ready to go. He grabbed them out of the fridge and tossed them on the counter.

Marci headed out the backdoor. He whistled and she stopped, turning with a smile.

"Where are you going?"

She looked innocent as a fox in a henhouse. Funny how a kid with blond braids and wide brown eyes could look so ornery. "I'm going to feed your dog."

He shook his head. "Not that cookie you have in your pocket."

No, he hadn't seen a cookie, but he knew how she worked. He'd been in her life a long time.

"Okay, no cookie." And out the door she went.

"She's cute." Katie shoved water bottles in the pack he'd put on the counter. "Are you okay?"

Her back was to him and she didn't turn to ask the question. Probably because she knew she was overstepping the boundaries, or something to that effect. He had invited her on a picnic, but he hadn't invited her into his life. Or Marci's life.

"Why do you ask?" Not exactly the "back off" response he'd planned.

But then, he'd invited her today. He'd put her squarely in his life. He'd enjoyed the subtle scent of oriental perfume that had lingered in his truck, a reminder of her presence. And because of that, he'd extended an invitation that had taken him by surprise. He probably wasn't the only one questioning the invite.

She added the sandwiches to the pack. "You looked a little lost for a few minutes. I just thought… I'm sorry, it isn't any of my business."

"No, I guess it isn't." He sighed and brushed a hand through his hair.

"Marci, she's your…"

"Goddaughter," he offered the one detail. "And it isn't really something I can discuss right now. But I appreciate that you asked."

The backdoor opened, ending the conversation. Maybe God would hear this one prayer of his—that Lulu Jenson would be okay and that he wouldn't have to break Marci's heart. As they headed out the back door, a hand brushed his. The touch took him by surprise and when he glanced Katie's way he thought maybe it took her by surprise, too. What stunned him more than the touch was that the simple gesture, her fingers against his, made him want to be less of a rock, handling everything on his own.

Once, a long time ago, he'd thought he'd be married, have kids, and have someone to be a partner in the tough times. It hadn't happened, obviously. And it had convinced him there weren't many women interested in a relationship that included a child that wasn't even his.

It had been a long time since he'd trusted.

Chapter Four

They shared a picnic on the banks of the lake, horses tied nearby and the border collie, Jake, nosing in the brown grass of early October. Nearby, a stream trickled, the water emptying into the lake. There had been a good rain a few days ago, which had set the nearly dry source of water into action once again. He told her that come spring, when the snows melted, it would be more of a rush rather than a trickle of water.

Katie had listened, watching as Marci wandered away to walk along the lake, playing with the dog as she went.

"So, you don't ride or fish. What do you do for fun in Missoula?" Cord asked as he leaned back on the blanket, a careful eye on Marci.

What did she do in Missoula? Katie shrugged one shoulder as she searched for an answer because in the last year she'd changed a lot. She no longer partied. She no longer cared about the dating scene. She doubted he wanted those answers. He was being polite, not really wanting insight into her life. "I work."

One corner of his mouth kicked up. "Of course you do. What else? Do you date? Do you play bridge?"

She laughed at that. "People still play bridge?"

"I have no idea. It was just the first thing that came to mind."

"Bridge came to mind? I'm not sure what that says about you. Do you know how to play bridge?"

"Not a clue," he confessed, his cheeks turning a little pink under his deep tan. "I know that we're trying to rebuild a bridge and hoping this wedding brings enough business to town to aid in that goal. I take it that's the wrong kind of bridge?"

"Yes, the wrong bridge."

"So," he prodded again.

"I work. I spend time with friends." Most of whom were getting married or moving away. That left fewer friends. She did have a collection of never-to-be-worn-again bridesmaid's dresses hanging in her closet.

"Family?"

"Nothing like yours."

"Is Gwen your only sibling?"

She glanced at him, a sideways glance, taking in his handsome profile half shaded by the black cowboy hat he had donned after church. "Yes, she is."

He had been leaning back on one elbow. He sat up, watching her. She chose to look toward the lake because it was easier to focus on water that shimmered and sparkled than to face his piercing blue eyes, softened as they were by dark lashes. On the bank of the lake Marci picked up a rock and skipped it across the glassy water.

"You're close, you and Gwen?" Cord pushed.

"We're close." Enough. They were close enough.

"Your parents?"

She looked away from Marci back to the man sitting next to her. "Are they close?"

He grinned and her insides melted a little. "Sure, okay, we'll go with that."

"They've been married for thirty-three years and they wouldn't not be married. But I'm not sure if they like each other."

She sometimes wondered if they liked her. And she wasn't a melodramatic person, just a realist. She didn't fit. When she looked at family pictures she was the odd one out. Gwen, beautiful, petite, dark brown hair and a brain that never forgot a fact. Carla, her mother, was a dentist. James, her father, was a lawyer. Katie's red hair came from her great-grandmother. She'd once heard her mother say that she'd wanted Katie to have black hair, like her husband's.

"My parents were high school sweethearts," Cord said with a shrug. "I don't know how they stay in love but they do."

"They are proof that some marriages work."

"Yes, I guess they are. They've been a great example to us. We've seen them work out their disagreements, go through hard times and still hold on to each other."

Katie wondered, but she didn't comment. What she'd seen in the few days since she'd arrived in Jasper Gulch on the first day of October was a couple that loved each other but maybe weren't in agreement. There was something beneath the surface, something going on. Katie saw it in the looks they gave one another and in whispered conversations. If something was going on between Jackson and Nadine Shaw, it couldn't be easy to work through it with strangers in their home.

"Thank you for letting me join you today," Katie said, shifting to a safer topic. "I know this is usually your day with Marci."

He pushed his hat back and gave her a closer look. "You know that, do you?"

"Julie," she admitted.

"Julie, of course. She's a little too much in my business of late."

"She's really terrific."

"Of course she is. Terrific and in my business."

"I'm sorry." Katie pulled her knees up and rested her chin as she watched Marci race across the field, the dog chasing after her. "I didn't mean to pry."

"You're not prying. You've been tossed into our lives since you got here. I don't think that was your plan or our intention. And I'm probably as surprised as Julie that I invited you this afternoon. Or that Marci agreed to the invitation."

"Why is that?"

"That you've been tossed into our lives?" His smile said he knew that wasn't her question. "I think because you're easy to be around and you allow yourself to be a part of what is going on here."

"Not that."

His gaze now lingered on the young girl who was sitting on the grass some distance from them, the black-and-white border collie licking her face as she laughed. "I protect her because she deserves to be protected. I was engaged."

"I heard. But not to her mother?"

He shook his head but his attention remained focused on Marci. "I met my fiancée when Marci was four. Susan didn't want anything to do with Marci. I kept holding on to hope that she'd change her mind. I kept moving forward with the wedding plans, thinking that once we were married she would warm up to the idea of Marci in our lives. Instead, she left the state with my best friend."

"Dodged that one, didn't you?"

He laughed at her easy response to a situation that had left him with a bad taste in his mouth and no desire to ever repeat the mistake. "I guess you could put it that way."

"I do have a way with words."

"Yes, you do."

"And Marci's mom?"

He sighed and sat up, one leg bent, his knee up, the other leg stretched out in front of him. "Angie. She was one of my best friends for most of my life. She got pregnant in college by a guy who didn't want Marci."

His phone rang, ending the moment and the conversation. Katie started packing up the remains of their picnic as he pushed himself to his feet and walked away. As he talked in low tones, she cast a cautious glance his way, wondering what might have stolen the smile he wore just moments earlier. As he talked, he watched Marci playing, nodded a few times, and when the conversation ended, he didn't speak for a few minutes.

"Is everything okay?" She had everything back

in the backpack and the blanket they'd sat on was folded.

"No, I have to leave. And I'm not sure how I'm going to do this, but I can't take Marci to town with me."

"You have to go to town?"

He grabbed the pack and attached it to the saddle of his horse. "Yes, I do. There's a situation I need to take care of."

"Of course."

He untied her horse and led the gray gelding to her. They stood there for a moment, she staring up at him. It took her by surprise, having to look up. Her world closed in, focusing only on him. And it frightened her. She didn't want to go down that path again.

This man was dangerous. His strength was a danger. As was his kindness. More than that, his vulnerability was dangerous. That might be the most dangerous part, that part of him that had been hurt, might still be hurting, might need someone desperately. It was in his eyes, in the guarded look he shifted in Marci's direction as the girl cavorted with the dog, unaware of the phone call. Katie guessed that it probably had something to do with the child.

She wanted to help Cord but wasn't sure how. And she knew better than to try to be that person for anyone. Because it always hurt later, when she realized she'd just been filling the space of friend.

He handed her the reins to the horse.

"Foot in the stirrup," he said softly, and as she moved, she realized how close they were to one another. His hand was on the saddle and their faces were inches apart. He leaned, so close she could feel the warmth of him.

He stepped back, shaking his head just a little.

"Wow." He whistled. "I'm not sure what to say."

"Hmm." She didn't know what to say, either. She needed to think of something. Fast. Before she claimed the kiss she knew he'd considered and then reconsidered. "What is the situation in town, or should I ask?"

"You shouldn't ask."

"Is there anything I can do?"

He darted a quick look over his shoulder before looking at her again, letting out a shaky sigh. "Her grandmother, Lulu, has Alzheimer's. I'm not sure how long she's had it, but it's progressed to the point that she can no longer hide it."

"Marci?"

Serious regret settled in the depths of his blue eyes. "We were going to sit her down and tell her. We should have told her sooner but it's a lot of reality for an eleven-year-old kid."

"And right now?"

"She was at the diner and when she walked out to the car she couldn't remember how to get home. She looked confused, so a couple of friends asked if they could help and she told them. They took her home and are there with her now, waiting for me."

"We're wasting time."

She somehow she managed to get back in the saddle, knowing her legs would punish her later for this unusual treatment. Marci was heading their way, laughing as the dog chased her. Cord had her horse untied and handed her the reins when she stopped in front of him.

"Time to go, kiddo."

Marci threw herself easily into the saddle and gave him an annoyed look from her perch on the pretty bay she rode, a deep brown–coated animal with black legs and a black mane and tail. Until today Katie hadn't known a bay from a dapple gray. Gray being the horse she rode.

"Why?"

"We need to take Katie back to the main ranch and then you and I will have a talk." Cord had a hand on her horse's neck.

"About?" Marci held the reins of the restless horse and finally spoke sharply, telling her mare to stop. The mare settled.

"I don't want to discuss it right now." Cord's tone took on that fatherly, brook-no-argument tone.

"Is something wrong with Grammy?"

Katie bit down on her lip and waited for Cord's reply. This man she'd known for only a few days, and already she felt so tied into his life. Her heart ached for him and for the girl staring him down. He might think that Marci didn't know anything was wrong with her grandmother, but Katie thought he might be wrong.

Now what did he do? Cord looked down at the ground, wishing it would swallow him up but knowing this was a situation he'd have to face. He looked up and caught the eyes of the woman he'd invited along for a day that should have been relaxing and now she was all kinds of tied into their lives. Exactly where he didn't want her.

"Why do you think something is wrong with your grammy?"

Marci bit down on her bottom lip and her sigh hung up a little, sounding more like a sob. "Because I know she's sick. I know something is wrong. She forgot the car in town and walked home. When I asked her where the car was, she told me she'd never owned a car."

"Why didn't you tell me?" Cord stood next to her horse, his hand on hers.

"Because later she remembered and she was embarrassed and told me it must be the blood pressure medication. But it wasn't, because she forgot that I go to school. I think she thought I was my mom."

Behind him, hooves crunched on the rocky ground. "If you want," Katie said, "I don't mind riding along. You'll get there quicker if you don't have to take me to the main house."

He glanced up at the woman in the saddle, her red hair was pulled back in a ponytail. Her cheeks were rosy from the cool, October mountain air and her green eyes were bright and knowing.

He didn't know what to say. He'd dragged her into their lives. He'd put her on that horse she rode with natural grace even though she'd never really ridden. He'd given her entrance and now he couldn't push her back. Because, man, he didn't want to face this alone. If she was willing to be a friend to both him and Marci during a pretty rotten time, he'd take the offer.

He didn't want to tell a kid that her grandmother was going to start forgetting her, forgetting school programs and forgetting hugs they had always shared.

He hated this disease, hated what it did to the person who faced it and the families that lost loved ones long before they left this earth. Eleven was too young to face this.

"Cord?" Her hand settled on his shoulder.

He looked up and finally nodded. "Marci, we'll check on Grammy together."

"Okay." Tears were filling Marci's brown eyes. "It isn't her medicine, is it?"

"No." He let out a long sigh. "It isn't."

As he swung himself into the saddle of his horse, Katie rode up next to Marci, putting her hand on his goddaughter's arm and giving her an encouraging smile. And Cord didn't know how to tell her she didn't have to do this. She'd stayed because her sister asked and now she was going to be with him when he told Marci that soon her grandmother would probably have to live in the nursing home a town away from them.

His big dun sidestepped beneath him, sensing his mood. The mousy-gray horse tossed his head and pulled at the bit, trying to move forward. Cord held him in careful control, watching as Katie and Marci rode out ahead of him. Life shifted, changing in that moment in a way he hadn't expected. He was still trying to tell himself that Katie was safe, an easy person to be around, uncomplicated. And then he called himself a liar because she was anything but uncomplicated.

When they pulled up to the little house Marci lived in with her grandmother, Cord noticed Lulu on the front porch sitting on her little glider bench. She waved and even smiled, but the smile faltered and her hand dropped to her lap.

Ten years ago he'd stood on this same porch wondering how to knock, how to tell Lulu that her only child was dead, killed when a truck slid on icy roads and hit her car head-on. He'd stayed the night, holding little Marci and promising the two of them that he'd always be there.

He remembered trying to explain that to Susan, his former fiancée. She'd told him that was fine but once they were married he'd have to understand that he couldn't take care of the whole world. They would have children of their own, she'd informed him, and a life of their own. He'd understood. He really had. A woman didn't want to share her life with an orphaned child and a widow.

He'd been prepared to juggle his responsibilities and he'd hoped Susan would come around. As he got out of the truck, Katie was getting out on the other side. She held the door open for Marci and reached for the child's hand. Marci took the offered hand without hesitation. And now he knew his other fear, that a girl growing into her teen years needed more than a bachelor cowboy.

Today she needed someone soft, someone with arms that could hug. She needed a gentle touch and a woman's voice in her ear. That had been obvious on the drive to town. Marci had held tight to Katie's hand as he had explained what was happening to her grandmother. It had surprised him that it was a stranger's hand Marci reached for, but maybe it made sense. Sometimes it was easier to turn to a stranger, someone with no expectations.

"It'll be okay." Katie offered as they walked toward the house. "But it won't be easy."

Honesty. It would not, in any way, be easy. He'd known for a while that something was up with Lulu. He'd seen it months before she'd told him the truth. He'd caught her a few times at church talking to someone she'd always known, but the look in her eyes had troubled him. It had been as if she was talking to strangers but pretending she knew them.

When he'd talked to his mom about this, she had told him that Alzheimer's patients often pretended to remember. She'd volunteered at the nursing home and understood better than he did.

"Marci!" Lulu stood as they approached. "Honey, I was worried about you. Where have you been?"

"With Cord, Grammy, remember? We saw him at church and I left with him."

Lulu frowned but then she nodded, "Of course. Do you know, I had to get a ride home with the Parkers? My car wouldn't start. But they're leaving now."

Marci looked from her grandmother to Cord. He nodded toward the house and she hurried inside, Katie right behind her. The door closed with a soft click, leaving Cord and Lulu alone on the porch.

"Lulu?" Cord took her arm. "Let's go inside."

"No, Cord, I don't want to do this."

"We have to."

She shook her head and then she sobbed into his shoulder. Her tears were damp and warm against his sleeve. "If we don't say it, it won't be real."

She'd said the same thing ten years ago. She'd cried when she saw him on the front porch and she'd told him not to tell her. She'd begged him to go away and not be the one to do this to her. But he'd taken her by the arm and led her inside and he'd told her anyway. He'd told her that her only child had died in a car accident.

"You don't have to do this, Cord. You don't always have to be the one."

He laughed a little because she sniffled and looked up at him, smiling. "I wish that wasn't true, Lulu."

"Please, just one more day of normal."

"What's normal anyway, Lulu?"

She sobbed again. "Normal is waking up in the morning and knowing your granddaughter's name and why she's in your home. I want more of those days."

He wasn't ashamed of the hot sting of tears in his eyes. He swiped at them and leaned to kiss the top of her head. "I know."

"Promise me you'll take care of her."

"Lulu, I already promised. I signed on the dotted line two weeks ago, remember?"

"Yes, I remember. Don't patronize me, you big ox."

He laughed because laughing hurt a lot less than crying. "You always say such sweet things, Lu."

"I know I do." She reached for the front door. "I don't know what we'll say to her. How do we explain?"

"We'll figure it out together." He reached for the door and they stepped inside, Lulu holding his arm as he led her to her green upholstered rocking chair.

She held her arms out to Marci. "Come here, sweetie."

Marci fled the room.

"Marci." In answer, Cord heard a door slam.

Lulu reached for his hand. "Give her a minute. And tell me, who's your pretty little friend?"

Katie didn't run. Instead, she knelt down in front of Lulu, taking both of the trembling, frail hands in hers. "I'm not really a friend, Mrs.

Jenson. I'm here because my sister is getting married. I'm staying with the Shaws."

"Why aren't you getting married?"

"Because no one has asked me and because I think it's easier to be single."

"Posh, that's the silliest thing I've ever heard. I wish you would marry Cord. He's going to need someone."

"He has a big family and he loves Marci."

"I know he does," Lulu shook her head. "We need to talk to Marci."

"I'll go get her," Katie offered.

He knew it was a coward's way out, but Cord let her. "First door on the left."

When she walked through the door, he stayed close, listening. He heard Katie, a stranger, telling Marci that Cord would always be there for her. She told Marci how blessed she was to have so many people who cared about her. And that she would still have her grandmother. It might not be the same, but they would have each other and they would even have moments when nothing felt wrong.

And then she told Marci a story about a neighbor that she still visited in the nursing home. Sometimes the neighbor remembered her, sometimes she didn't. But the hugs were still the same. The smile was the same. And they sang songs together and her neighbor always remembered the words. The songs helped the neighbor remember Katie and other details of her life.

"Does your grandmother have a favorite song, Marci?"

"'In the Sweet By and By,'" the girl responded in a voice that trembled.

"Then make that song your memory together, Marci. Sing it with her every day and every time you can be together later, and it will be your connection. She'll remember that song."

Cord leaned a hip against the wall and thanked God above that Katie Shaw had happened into their town and into their lives. Even if she didn't stay long, he had a feeling they would be grateful that she stayed.

Chapter Five

Katie felt a little lost in the big ranch house that belonged to the Shaw family. Nadine had been nothing but kind, showing her around, telling her to help herself to anything she needed. Katie knew where the coffee and filters were kept so that she could make coffee. She knew that the pantry was stocked with cereal and there were homemade pancakes in the freezer that could be reheated in the toaster. Everyone had been kind and welcoming to the stranger in their midst. Even the couples who were taking part in the big wedding had included her.

But still, she was a stranger in someone else's home, living in one of their bedrooms, eating their food. And because Gwen had asked. And then Gwen had gone back to work. Such was Katie's life. Her work wasn't important, not like Gwen's. She ran a clothing store. She wasn't going to deliver babies or keep pregnant women healthy.

She didn't know if anyone would ever love her as anything more than a friend. And she was so tired of trying to make someone love her—by being friendly, funny, one of the guys, or any of the other ways she had tried to get attention.

On the front porch of the Shaw house she watched the sun climbing on the eastern horizon and she thought about the previous day when Cord Shaw had sat down with Lulu and her granddaughter and discussed what Alzheimer's would do to Marci's grandmother and how it would change their lives. She'd wanted to cry for the three of them. Later she'd wanted to hug the man who had taken it upon himself to be there for a friend's child and that friend's mother. Hugging that man, Cord Shaw, equaled danger in the highest degree. So she wouldn't. Ever.

A truck stopped in front of the house, the dust settling around it. The Shaw's cattle dog ran from the back of the house. Julie Shaw stepped out of the car, waved and headed her way.

"What are you up to today?" Julie leaned to run her hands through the dog's coat and then she pointed and the dog sat.

"Not much, I guess. I'm here as Gwen's proxy until she can escape residency for a few days. Her schedule is pretty tight and I had time off because I haven't taken a vacation in a couple of years."

Julie took hold of Katie's hand and led her through the front door. "I need to pick up some mail for my dad. Mayoral stuff, I think, and some copy for papers in nearby towns that will advertise the wedding and coming events. Do you want to go to town with me? I think it would be much better than shuffling around here looking for something to do."

"It would be great to go to town. I haven't really had a chance to explore."

At that, Julie laughed. "I promise, you won't have much to explore. A museum that isn't finished, the library and a broken-down bridge that hasn't been repaired since the town's heyday, really."

"Because of an accident?" Katie followed Julie to the kitchen and watched as the woman, only slightly younger than herself with hair more auburn than red, poured a cup of coffee.

She knew from Lilibeth Shoemaker, purveyor of local gossip, that Julie was engaged to a cowboy who had come to town for the rodeo in July. Julie and Ryan Travers were one of the local couples getting married at the end of the month.

Julie faced her holding a cup of steaming coffee in her hands. "Yes, the accident. My great-great-aunt Lucy Shaw ran off the bridge in her Model T, back in 1926. They never found her body and of course the whole incident shook everyone up."

"I can imagine. But why not repair the bridge?"

Julie shrugged one shoulder and lifted the cup to take a sip. "Because people are funny and they get ideas they can't let go of. The bridge ended Lucy Shaw's life. The bridge might bring the world and the world's problems right to our proverbial doorstep and we wouldn't want that."

Katie didn't know how to respond and then Julie smiled.

"Ah, so we are keeping the world at bay?" Katie asked.

"Something like that. Or maybe we're holding on to old grudges. I hope they can all work it out and that's why we have the Bridge Builders. They're the committee in town that is tasked with ideas on how to rebuild. But I think they are also building bridges in the community, trying to get everyone on the same page. But we shouldn't talk about—"

"Julie." The word of warning came from the doorway. Katie turned, smiling a hesitant smile at her host, Jackson Shaw. In this room with just herself and Julie, he seemed bigger than life with his silvery-gray hair and strong personality so evident.

“I’m teasing, Daddy.” Julie set her cup down and went to give him a hug that eased his frown into a half smile. “But you know that people in our little town do hold on to some grudges.”

“Maybe so.” Jackson poured himself a cup of coffee and then glanced around the room. “Where’s your mother?”

“Not in here. You don’t know where she is?”

He shook his head but didn’t respond. Instead, he sipped the hot coffee and grabbed a biscuit off a plate on the counter.

“Maybe she went to the store.” He shifted away from the counter, his expression easing. “I guess Wes Middleton is doing a little better and coming in to the store once in a while, but Rosemary is still running the show.”

“And being the purveyor of gossip and goodwill. Her gift.” Julie said it with a smile.

“Not a gift I want you to have.” His voice was gruff and he leaned to kiss his daughter on the brow. “I’d love to stay and chat with you girls, but we’re tagging some calves this afternoon.”

Julie glanced from her father to Katie. “Ear tags, kind of like putting a name tag on a dog. It becomes the calf’s identity.”

“Got it.” Katie smiled at Mr. Shaw. “Is there anything I can do?”

“No, you enjoy your stay here at the ranch. I

hear Helen, our wedding coordinator, left us and Cord is trying to put you to work. See that you stand your ground."

"Thank you, sir, I will."

He gave her a curt nod and with that he was gone, grabbing a black cowboy hat off the hook by the door as he walked out.

Julie watched him go and Katie wondered at the troubled look in her eyes.

"Is everything okay?"

Julie turned, smiling again. "Of course, I'm just a little worried. I can't recall my parents ever losing track of each other. They've been this way for a few months and I'm not sure why."

"All couples have their troubles."

The conversation ended with the arrival of the Shaws' housekeeper. Julie hugged the older woman whom Katie had easily become fond of in the past few days.

"You know you missed breakfast." Sandy opened a drawer and filled it with kitchen towels she'd carried in with her.

"I made breakfast this morning." Julie went on in a conversational tone. "Oh, and I need to know how to make your casserole, the one with beef and peppers."

Sandy's eyebrows rose as her eyes widened and she stepped back. Her eyes danced with amusement as she surveyed the youngest Shaw. "You cooked?"

"Yes, of course I did."

"And you're still alive to talk about it."

Julie looked a little hurt, but the twinkle in her eyes said otherwise. She brushed auburn curls over her shoulder. "I'm a work in progress, Sandy."

At that, Sandy laughed. "You sure are and I'll print off all your favorite recipes so that when you and your young man are married, you can impress him with your culinary skills."

"And maybe sometimes you could just come over to my place and cook for me?"

The housekeeper shook her head, but Katie got the impression that she'd do anything for Julie Shaw.

They left shortly after that, with Julie driving down the bumpy road. The radio was on and Julie kept up a steady stream of conversation about her business, Warm and Fuzzy, and her relationship with Ryan Travers.

"Do you want to eat at Great Gulch Grub?" Julie asked as they drove into the small town situated in a picturesque valley, mountains rising in the distance, snow-covered at the tops. Montana the way it was meant to be, thought Katie. She'd lived in Montana since her preteen years. But she hadn't spent time in small towns that dotted the state. She hadn't spent nearly enough time enjoying Big Sky country without city streets and suburbs.

"That sounds good. I've heard it has the best pies."

"Homemade," Julie concurred.

They drove in on Shaw Boulevard and turned right on the wide main street, parking immediately in front of the diner.

"Wow, we're lucky to find a parking space," Julie announced as she pocketed her keys and opened the door. "Let's go to city hall first. I think Cord is there. He's on the city council and I think Dad has him busy on the Centennial Committee work as well as the wedding."

Katie stepped onto the sidewalk and followed Julie back across Shaw Boulevard and then across Main Street to the opposite side. She glanced up and down the street and her gaze settled on the empty store she'd seen when they first came to town.

"Is that building for rent?"

Julie turned to look. "Yes, as a matter of fact, Cord owns it. He bought a couple of empty buildings, hoping that in time we'd bring in new business."

The "why" look Julie gave her went unanswered because Katie didn't really have an answer. She had a dream, not real plans. And as she followed the other woman, Katie's plans grew. She loved the sweaters that Julie sold mainly online. Of course, other women would feel the same way and want to buy them locally. She imagined a store, the one she'd always dreamed of owning, with women's clothing, accessories. Just a dream.

The city hall and chamber of commerce were located in what appeared to be an old bank building. Like so many of the stores, the front was sided with wood. A shingled awning gave a small amount of cover. Katie looked up and down the street, taking in a police station, bakery, veterinarian's office and a beauty salon called the Cutting Edge.

"Oh, a salon. Do they do nails?" Katie looked at her hands because before wedding time a manicure was going to be in order. And she had a feeling if there was only one salon in Jasper Gulch it would be a busy place.

"They have a girl who comes in a couple of times a week. She doesn't do a lot of business in Jasper Gulch, so she alternates between several small towns."

"She's going to be popular before the wedding. I wonder if she has friends who would want to set up the day before the wedding to take care of manicures for any of the brides that might want one. And, of course, hair, there will be women wanting their hair done."

Julie reached for the door of the city hall. "You're Cord's answer to a prayer, aren't you? He's been dreading this wedding and now he has someone who can get him through the next month without his going crazy. I can guarantee he wouldn't have thought about details like hairstylists and manicurists."

Heat settled in Katie's cheeks and she moved her hands to her face. "I'm sorry, I shouldn't take over. I think I even told him I would help, but I'm not a wedding coordinator."

Julie laughed at that. "I really don't think he'll mind if you take over some of the details."

"Are you talking about me for some reason?" Cord asked from behind the counter as they walked into the building with its high ceilings, big windows and dark, polished wood.

"Katie is planning out loud, for the wedding." Julie walked through a gate and stepped behind the counter. She gave her brother an easy kiss on the cheek. "Don't overwork her, though. She deserves a little time to see the sights."

"I don't plan on overworking anyone," Cord insisted, handing his sister a file. "Except you. I have some ideas for revamping your website. I shoved the notes in with the advertisements that need to be taken care of. I've been calling radio and television stations to make sure we'll have at least some media here at the end of the month."

"You think of everything, brother mine." Julie stepped away from him. "What else did you have planned for today?"

"I'm not sure, but I think some photos for the wedding. Vintage photographs to hang in the reception hall." His blue eyes shifted from his sister to Katie and it unsettled her, that look with the easy smile.

"I've been thinking about this," Katie admitted, and then she bit down on her lip and shrugged. "I'm sorry, it isn't my wedding or my place."

Cord extended his hand, giving her the floor. "No, you go ahead. My idea of marriage probably is a little less romantic than yours."

She didn't really have romantic feelings about weddings, but she didn't tell him that. "What if we find vintage wedding pictures, scan and enlarge them? We can use them in the decor for the reception, but also the brides could be photographed holding the vintage photos."

Julie squealed and clapped her hands. "As a bride, I love that idea. I could have a photo enlarged of my great-great-grandmother Elaine and have my picture taken holding it. Maybe the brides who can would want to bring pictures of their own relatives."

"I like that idea." Cord came out from behind the counter, and Katie didn't have time to steady herself before he gathered her in a tight hug and kissed her cheek.

He stilled and then his arms moved, releasing her. She looked up, meeting that steady blue gaze of his, wishing she'd see laughter. Instead, other emotions flickered across his face. Shock. Yes, she definitely saw shock in his eyes.

Katie shot a look in Julie's direction and saw the same surprised expression on her face. Katie shrugged it off, because she was used to this, to men who treated her like a sister or a friend.

She definitely didn't want Cord to think of her as a little sister. But tumbling into complicated emotions for someone like him was also not something she needed. The past year of her life had been less complicated due to her no-dating policy. She hadn't been overlooked, stood up or forgotten when someone else came along.

She felt more at ease because she wasn't chasing after love. She was waiting for the right person to find her.

She never again wanted to hear the words *"Katie, I thought we were just friends."*

Neither of them had to let this be a "thing" between them, though. Chemistry happened to people all the time. It was unexpected but not the end of the world. Really.

Katie swallowed, pasted a smile on her face and plunged forward. "So let's go find some photos."

"We can start by seeing what Robin Frazier has unearthed in her genealogical research," Julie offered, further breaking the uncomfortable moment.

Katie had been introduced to Robin in passing at the reception the first night in town. Robin was doing genealogical research for her master's and the trail had led her to Jasper Gulch. She'd been in town for several months, Katie had been told.

"Lead the way." Katie jumped at the chance to look at the photos, and the opportunity to be distracted.

"It isn't far to lead. She has a, well, basically a closet at the back of the building." Cord motioned Katie through the gate. "I think Olivia Franklin is in there helping put stuff together. She's worked at a historical museum so we're pretty happy she came back to town when she did."

Julie bumped a shoulder into Katie's. "We're not as happy she came back as Jack McGuire is. They're joining us in the fifty-couple march down the aisle."

More happy couples, just what Katie needed.

Cord shook his head as he followed his sister and Katie through the gate. What a mistake, hugging the pretty redhead who had fallen into his life. He could chalk it up as spontaneous and grateful, because she'd come to his rescue twice in the past two days. Yesterday she'd saved him in the situation with Marci and Lulu. She'd known what to say to Marci, a child he'd known her entire life, whom he'd helped to raise.

"Did you find someone to help Marci and her grandmother?" Katie asked, glancing back at him as he stepped forward to open the door to the small room being used to put the museum together, or at least the beginning stages of a museum.

"Yes, we did." He shot his sister a look because he saw surprise all over her face. "A retired nurse is going to stay with them for a bit, just to make sure things run smoothly. I'm hoping Lulu won't have to be put in a nursing home. At least for a while."

"I hope that's the case."

"Did I miss something?" Julie jumped into the conversation.

"Lulu had a spell yesterday." Cord sighed, knowing *spell* didn't quite explain. "Her dementia is getting worse."

Julie touched his arm. "I'm so sorry, Cord."

"So am I. There isn't much we can do about it."

"No, but you have to remember you have family to help."

Cord nodded, wanting to let the subject go because Katie was already being yanked into their lives a little too far and maybe she didn't have to be all the way in.

They entered the room where he knew Robin Frazier and Livvie had been working most of the morning. Robin was alone in the room. He glanced around, but in a room this small, it wasn't as if Livvie could be hiding. Robin had photographs in her hand and a look on her face that Cord didn't quite get. It was somewhere between guilty and unsure. He didn't want to be the suspicious one, but there was something about Robin Frazier and he couldn't quite figure it out.

He'd like to know before his dad tried to marry her off to one of his younger brothers. Adam and Austin were being cautious with all the matchmaking going on. And good thing they were.

"Find something interesting?" He stepped forward, flanked by his sister and Katie.

Robin spread photographs across the table she'd been working at. "Not really interesting. Well, I don't know. I just noticed that in every photo I've found, Silas Massey wore the same suit. Why?"

Cord shrugged it off. "Maybe he had more than one suit but all the same style?"

Julie stepped closer, fingering the pictures. She lifted one and gave it a careful look. "I heard that he didn't have the ability with money that Ezra Shaw had. Maybe he wanted to look the part of wealthy businessman? He had a reputation to uphold, after all."

Next to him, Katie picked up a few pictures. "Is this Lucy?"

Cord took the picture from her. "Yes. That's the car that went over the bridge, too."

"You all look so much alike. It's the eyes. Even in the black-and-white photos, you all have very distinct eyes." Katie held the photo up and looked at him. Cord met her gaze and he thought he could say the same about distinct eyes.

Hers.

They drew a guy in, even when he wasn't planning to be drawn. Those eyes, the color of a meadow in spring, flickered and glanced away. He had a real urge to turn her face so that he could look a little closer, feel a little more.

He shook it off, the way he did when he landed wrong on his knee, reinjuring what had happened years ago when he'd been going through a saddle-bronc phase.

Katie set the photo on the table and moved on, her bottom lip caught between her teeth as she sifted through the photos. He looked away, his attention focusing on Robin Frazier as she settled her hand on the same picture Katie had commented on. Shadows lurked in her blue eyes as she studied that picture and then pushed it to the side.

He started to say something, to ask if she

was okay, but he knew that sometimes a person needed space to figure out what they were looking for.

Katie didn't have a difficult time finding what she was looking for. Within thirty minutes she had a neat collection of wedding photos. She browsed the brides in their wedding finery, a faint smile playing at the corners of her pretty mouth.

He remembered the first night he'd met her, when her sister mentioned the wedding dress that had been their grandmother's. Katie had smiled and pretended everything was fine, but he'd seen the shadows in her green eyes at the mention of that dress.

It was the last thing he should have noticed about the woman standing across from him. Unfortunately, he kept noticing more and more about the sister of the bride.

The door opened and Olivia stepped in. He smiled at the tiny blonde he'd known most of his life. "Hey, Livvie. Sorry for invading."

Olivia shrugged it off. "The more the merrier. Looking for anything in particular?"

"We were looking for wedding photos to use for the wedding," Cord explained. "Is there anything the two of you need?"

Livvie shook her head. "Nothing but more space."

"Yeah, I hope we can give you that space soon.

Hey, Ethan mentioned the church bell. If it isn't going to be repaired, why couldn't we take it down and put it in the museum?"

Her eyes lit up. "That would be amazing."

"No promises," Cord said. "But I'll do my best."

"Do you ladies want to join Katie and me for lunch?" Julie asked as she headed for the door.

"I brought a sandwich." Livvie had already bent her head over some papers.

From her place next to Katie on the opposite side of the table, Robin shook her head but didn't look up. "No, I think I'll stay here and keep cataloguing photos. I've found that my research is coming in handy for the museum and there are a few ladies who are going to join me today to see if we can put together a one-hundred-year time line of photos. Or as close as we can get."

"If you find more wedding photos, I'd like to see them." Katie held the photos they'd found and Robin handed her a manila envelope. She slid them inside. "You're sure it's okay to take these?"

"I'm sure." Robin looked to Livvie. "Don't you think?"

"Definitely. I think they all have names on the back."

"Thank you." Katie held the envelope of photos and headed for the door.

"Anything else?" Livvie asked, her tone distracted.

Yeah, answers, Cord thought. About a lot of things. Again his gaze settled on Katie and he wondered why most of his questions went back to her. She was more interesting than Robin Frazier's family tree and even more interesting than the photos of Lucy and Ezra that seemed to have gotten lost in the piles of pictures on the table.

He watched the woman in question leave with his sister and he didn't follow because there were times in a man's life when he knew he had to remember his convictions. He needed to focus on this wedding, on Marci and Lulu, on any number of things. The things that would be in his life longer than a month. Katie was easy to be around; that didn't mean he had to be around her every minute of the day. As a matter of fact, just knowing that should have helped him realize he needed to spend less time in her presence.

Chapter Six

Two days later, Katie was back in town with Julie. She'd come to pick up photos that Rosemary at the store had sent off to be enlarged. And poor Julie was her only source of transportation. She wished she'd gone home, at least to get her own car. Maybe next week.

Julie had gone to the bank down the street and Katie wandered alone, content to check out the different businesses in town. She had already gone into the bakery to talk about wedding cake. The coordinator had taken care of the main cake design. Each couple would have their own small cake. The orders were placed, cake flavors, icing and colors had been chosen. It was a huge undertaking for such a small bakery and Katie had learned that some of the baking would have to take place at Great Gulch Grub. Better known as the café.

She stopped in front of the empty store she'd noticed before. It was small with a shingled awning and wide windows that gave passersby a decent view of the interior.

"Still looking at this store?" Julie walked up next to her. Katie smiled at the other woman's reflection standing next to hers in the window.

"Yes." She turned to face Julie. "I've always wanted a shop of my own. I've actually been saving."

"What would you carry?"

"Clothing." Katie stopped and with a shake of her head she backed away from the store. "It's a dream, nothing more."

"I had a dream when I was a kid. Dad bought me a few sheep for 4-H. The rest is history. Katie, sometimes a dream becomes our reality."

Katie smiled a little easier. "Thank you. It would be amazing, not just having the store but being able to live here."

"It would be amazing to be able to buy clothes in Jasper Gulch. I mean, we have the feed store."

"Feed store? Clothes?"

Julie laughed. "Well, jeans, work boots, gloves and work coats."

"Designer, I'm sure."

"Definitely," Julie agreed.

They turned as a truck honked. Cord's big Ford King Ranch pulled up to the curb. The passenger-side window rolled down and he leaned in that direction.

"I happen to know the guy who owns that building if you're interested in renting it."

Katie shook her head. "Just window-shopping."

"Well, let me know if you change your mind. Would you be interested in looking at the tent they set up today? I know we're three weeks out, but with all of the events coming up, we're moving ahead with the tents so that we can make sure we have plenty of room and plenty of time to prepare."

"Tents, just what she wants to do on a pretty day." Julie glanced at her watch. "I have to meet Ryan."

"I can give Katie a ride home. If that works for the two of you?"

Julie looked at Katie and she nodded in agreement. "That works."

What choice did she have? She didn't have a car, so she could either infringe on Julie's time with Ryan, or go with Cord. Cord, who had the rugged, handsome cowboy image all sewed up. And he smelled like mountains, fresh air and leather.

He leaned a little farther across the cab of the truck and the passenger-side door opened. Katie told Julie goodbye and climbed into the truck. She shot a cautious look at the man behind the wheel.

He happened to look at her at the same time. She would have been fine if he hadn't winked. But he did.

The fairgrounds were empty of crowds, of course. The rodeo arena was abandoned for the season. The festival hall was locked up tight. Cord's truck pulled up to a giant white tent. It actually appeared to be two tents pushed together.

"I hope we don't get a strong wind between now and the wedding," she said.

Cord pulled the keys from the truck ignition and pocketed them. "That's an optimistic thought. It matches mine. I hope it doesn't snow."

"Yikes, that would be bad."

"Very."

They got out of the truck and met in front of the tent opening. As they stepped inside, Katie was pulled back in time and she could see it. Maybe without the fifty couples. Maybe just one couple, candlelit chandeliers, Christmas lights and white tulle. Flowers. She didn't see dark fall colors but whites and muted autumn shades of yellow, burnt orange and red.

"You're glowing."

She looked up at the man next to her. "Glowing?"

"The sunlight coming through the tent canvas. And the look on your face. You are seeing it, aren't you? How it could look that night?"

"Can't you?"

"Afraid not. It's the guy gene."

She reached for his hand and led him inside. "I think you could put seating on both sides of the tent and have them angled toward the center, where the two tents are joined. The brides and grooms could come from two directions. That would give everyone the opportunity to see them. They could meet in the middle and split off. As the bride and groom meet, they would go to one side or the other. Together."

"I like that idea." He took hold of her hand. "So we would have them walk in, brides from one side and grooms from the other?"

"Yes, that's it."

"What about the bridesmaids and best, um, best men?"

"They'll walk in before the couples. I think they come down the center together and then form a half circle at the back of the tent. The brides and grooms will be in front of them, turning to face the guests. We can have Pastor Ethan stand facing the couples."

"Good, we'll give it a try. The couples who are in town are going to be here in less than an hour so they can look at the tent and get a feel for things."

"Then let's give this a try before they get here."

He let go of her hand and she missed the touch,

but she couldn't. She couldn't miss his touch. She couldn't want his touch. He backed away. "I'll go to the other side."

"To the back far corner. Come in diagonal toward the opposite corner."

She watched him walk away. When he was on the far side of the tent, she nodded. "Walk slowly. We have to meet at the same time."

He started walking. She watched, matching her steps to his. Sunlight did filter through the white canvas. The air inside was still but cool. The man walking toward her was not, repeat, *not* her groom. But her heart raced a little and it hurt to breathe.

They met at the front center of the tents and joined hands. She looked up at him and he wasn't smiling. "That's the first time I've actually made it down the aisle," he confessed.

"It's the first time I wasn't a bridesmaid."

"Interesting," he whispered.

Her heart agreed. And then he leaned, still holding her hand and his lips touched hers. His free hand moved to her back and his mouth lingered on hers. She couldn't resist moving her free hand to his hair, feeling the soft waves beneath her fingers. When his lips on hers stilled she moved back, parting from him, from the moment. He didn't let go of her hand.

"You may kiss the bride," he whispered close to her ear.

"I've never been anyone's bride, just the best friend."

"I've never managed to be the groom. But at least now I know how that kiss feels at the end."

She leaned into his shoulder, aware that their fingers were laced together and his hand was still on her back. "I don't think it counts."

"No, probably not. But it did help me to feel a little better about this wedding business. If we can create that same moment for the other couples."

She unlaced her fingers and stepped away. "I think they have to create their own moments."

His hands went behind his back and he looked around. "But we can help. We have to re-create the warmth of this light."

"Chandeliers with candles and Christmas lights."

"And no direct lighting inside, maybe just outside so that it glows through the canvas."

"Yes. And what about heat?"

"Hmm, yes, well..." He laughed a little. "I'm not cold, are you?"

"That isn't what I meant." She knew that he knew that.

He was too much. This situation was too much. She wanted to tell Gwen that it was her fault. The broken heart when Katie left would be Gwen's fault. Katie wouldn't do this again. She wouldn't be the friend, the buddy, the one who listened and helped, not to this man. She couldn't because she knew that it would hurt worse than it had ever hurt before.

Gwen! That reminded her. "My sister is coming back tomorrow. For the weekend. I think she's going to have her dress sized. Do you think we should have the brides meet with us on Saturday so we can make sure they've all picked a dress? We can have seamstresses here to make any adjustments."

"I'll call the people supplying the dresses and see if Saturday would work for them. I think they have seamstresses because they want the dresses adjusted a certain way. Don't ask, because I'm not into clothing."

"That would be great. And if the grooms and best men don't have suits, do you have someone providing those?"

"The same shop." He was still watching her and there was something about the way he studied her face. "About the dress, the one your sister is wearing..."

Katie stilled at his question. Her mind had been on the wedding preparations, an easy distraction. Now it was back on more personal things. The kind of things that hurt.

"Yes?"

He brushed a hand through his thick, dark hair and looked puzzled. And she didn't know why.

"I shouldn't have brought it up." He glanced at his watch.

"It's okay, just not something I want to talk about."

The sound of vehicles pulling up outside thankfully ended the conversation. A few minutes later, people streamed into the tents. The happy couples held hands as they walked around the interior of the tent. They talked amongst themselves. Their eyes glowed with happiness, with excitement, with promise.

And Katie felt a twinge that she didn't want to admit was envy. Envy because these people had found their special someone. They were going to have this wedding, even with the hype and the media, that would be wonderful. It would be soft lighting, beautiful dresses and romance.

Katie got the moment she always got, the rehearsal. Her heart ached because she was always the person standing in for the real bride. She was the bridesmaid. She was the best friend. She'd even taken the place once as best man to the groom, a childhood friend of hers.

She watched Cord approach the couples and gather them all together. There were thirty couples present, just over half of the fifty that would be marrying in less than three weeks. Cord motioned her forward and she joined the group, but she stood at the edge, not really a part of this experience, just a bystander.

"What we plan is for everyone to meet here at the Festival Hall on Saturday. We'll pick dresses, get them resized if needed. The men will meet me at the city hall where we will pick vintage suits of the same era that can be rented for the weekend. If you have a best man—and I know all of you don't—he can also choose a suit that day."

"What about bouquets?" one bride asked.

"The following Tuesday we'll be picking flowers." Cord looked to Katie. "Am I forgetting anything?"

"I'll have to look at your list to see what all has been done."

He grinned and his eyebrows shot up. "Does this mean you're my new wedding coordinator?"

"Wait a minute, what happened to the wedding coordinator?" A sharp female voice broke from the back of the crowd.

Katie looked through the group and spotted the woman. The pretty blonde dropped her groom's hand and stepped forward. Katie had almost announced that she wasn't the wedding coordinator, just a volunteer. Now, for Cord's sake, she kept her mouth shut.

* * *

Cord watched the woman approach and he nearly groaned. It was the bridezilla that was staying at Jasper Gulch's one hotel. She pointed a finger at him and narrowed her eyes. He really felt for her potential groom. A quick glance in that direction and he saw the unfortunate guy cringe.

"You said that all the details were being taken care of by a wedding coordinator. I looked up her credentials and she was good. She's done some beautiful weddings. I only agreed to this because I knew it was the only way to get a wedding planned by someone with her skill. Where is she now?"

Cord cleared his throat and went for calm, patient and not the guy who wished this woman would decide to leave town. "Our wedding coordinator was volunteering her time. Unfortunately, she was offered a better opportunity, a job that actually paid. I have all the notes she left with the details she had planned. And I have a new coordinator."

He shot Katie a look. He wondered how "hopeful" looked on him. Or would it be more like pleading? Whatever the look, she nodded and when she did, he turned back to the crowd of couples.

"She isn't a coordinator, but she has experience in the fashion industry."

"As in, she's what?" Bridezilla asked. From the back of the crowd he heard the overwhelmed groom call her name, Andrea, and ask her to please calm down. Cord couldn't agree more.

"Andrea, is it?" Katie stepped forward, her smile easy and calming. Cord hoped it worked on the brides because it was working on him. How could a person not believe everything would be okay when faced with that serene look?

"Yes, it's Andrea." Her voice was still sharp. Cord guessed not everyone felt the calming influence of Katie Archer.

"I'm not a wedding coordinator. I work in retail, in a clothing store. I have studied fashion and merchandising. We're going to work together to make this wedding beautiful. Everything you've ever hoped for."

"I doubt that." Andrea stomped off.

Katie continued, explaining other details. As she finished, thirty couples applauded. Well, minus one. Cord couldn't help feeling a surge of pride because Katie was...No, not his. She was the person who would probably save this wedding, though. She glanced his way and he nodded. He took over again.

"If you all could be here Saturday at two, we'll take care of dresses and bouquets. We'll also do a practice run-through on the ceremony."

He spent a few minutes discussing the arrangement, explaining how the couples would come into the tent. As he discussed the walk down the aisle, his gaze traveled to Katie. She stood to the side, talking quietly to couples, including Julie and Ryan, who had arrived late. Livvie and Jack were also in the group. Hannah and Brody had called and begged off because one of the twins, maybe both, had a virus.

Another half hour of wedding planning passed. When the group dispersed, he realized he was alone. He walked outside and looked around, finally spotting Katie in the area where the time capsule had been buried. Or should have been buried. He headed her way, realizing she wasn't alone. Rusty Zidek stood next to her; the former baseball player was ninety-six and just as wiry as ever.

"I wondered where you'd gotten off to," he said as he walked up to the two.

Rusty reached for Cord's hand. Rusty might be almost to his own centennial mark, but he still had a firm grip and a look in his eyes that said he didn't miss much. If anything.

"Rusty was telling me more about the history of the town. I guess it's your history, too. Both of yours."

"It's our history and our future. That time capsule meant a lot to this town." Rusty, with his cowboy hat covering gray hair and his always shaggy mustache, stepped close to where the capsule had been buried.

"If we never find it, we'll survive. We've survived worse things, Rusty." Cord knew the capsule had been important. But historical artifacts wouldn't make or break a town.

Rusty shook his head at Cord's easy words. "I know we'll make it, Cord. But that capsule would have been good for this town."

"Do you know what was in the capsule, Rusty?"

He shook his head. "I was just hoping it might bring a Massey or two back for the centennial. I would like to see this town growing. I'd like for it to be a place that people move to and that the younger generations don't give up on. There isn't much here for a young person starting out."

"I know, Rusty."

Rusty removed his hat and ran a hand through his hair. He managed a sheepish smile. "You know, it's good that we're doing this celebration. How's your dad, Cord? I know he's staying busy and I'd say he's more than a little worried about this time capsule situation."

"He's well, Rusty. I think it's been rough on everyone, made people a little suspicious in general. But we'll manage and hopefully we'll find that time capsule. I can't imagine why anyone would want to steal history."

"No, it doesn't make much sense, does it? Poor

ole Pete, and then Lilibeth getting eyed as the culprits. I think a few people might have blamed me if they thought they'd get away with it."

"It sure didn't bring out the best in us," Cord cautioned.

"No, it didn't. But this centennial is undoing some of those bad feelings." Rusty shifted, smiling at Katie. "But all this talk about time capsules and feuding isn't making Miss Archer feel at all like someone who wants to stay in Jasper Gulch. You give us a chance, Miss Archer. You'll find we're a decent bunch."

"I already believe that, Mr. Zidek."

"Call me Rusty." He scratched the back of his neck and gave the location of the time capsule one last look. "Well, you kids have a good afternoon. I'm going to head to the café and have an early dinner."

Rusty headed toward his ATV mule, his vehicle of choice in good weather. He gave them a casual wave as he climbed in and headed off, taking the dirt road out of the fairgrounds.

"Did someone actually think he took the time capsule?" Katie asked as they headed toward Cord's truck.

"If they did, they didn't say anything to me."

"He had a point, why would anyone want to steal a time capsule? They're typically, what, old newspapers, some photos and information about what was happening at the time?"

"Yes, that's the gist of it. I'm not sure why anyone would want to steal this thing."

Silence for a few more minutes. He unlocked his truck and opened the door for her. As she got in, she gave him a puzzled look.

"What?" he asked as she sat there, her gaze shifting back to the capsule area.

"Maybe there was something in there that the thief didn't want anyone to see?"

He chuckled at that. "Well, then that would point back to Rusty, because who else is still alive that could have been around when it was buried? What do you think might have been in it, a secret of some type?"

She wrinkled her nose at him and he took a step closer, unable to resist. She pushed against his shoulder. "You never know. Maybe there was something in there about a founder of the town, or a newspaper article that might have made someone look bad? A scandal."

"That's a thought, one I don't think any of us have come up with."

"It was just a thought, not something you should take too seriously."

He reached for her hand. "And what if you're right? If we can find out what was in that capsule, it would help."

"If I'm right, maybe they'll never find the time capsule and someone's secret. Would that be so bad?"

He wanted to kiss her again. It was the brightness of her green eyes, the way she'd thought about the capsule and even the fictional person with the secret to hide. He knew better than to follow through on another kiss. She'd walked into his life a week ago as one of the easiest women to be around. A woman who would only be in town a few weeks. With his dad pushing every single female inside the city limits of Jasper Gulch his way, Katie was a breath of fresh air.

He didn't want to ruin that for either of them.

"We shouldn't have kissed." Katie's words shook him loose from memories of the two times the wedding had almost been his.

"No, we shouldn't have." He wasn't about to apologize, though.

She leaned forward, taking him by surprise. And she didn't kiss him. She straightened his collar and then placed a cool hand on his cheek.

"I don't want to be that kind of friend, Cord. I'm looking for someone to spend my life with and not a casual relationship."

"Ouch." But it didn't hurt, it made him respect her more.

"It would make things difficult, and what if I do rent that building from you?"

"You're right, it would complicate things."

"Yes, definitely. Especially now that I seem to be the new wedding coordinator."

Her hand had moved from his cheek and he took a step back, preparing to close the door. "Yes, I didn't really plan that."

"No, I didn't think you did."

"I know you have other commitments."

"Close the door, I'm getting cold. And use that handy button to start this truck."

Cord hit the remote and started to close the door. "Katie, it doesn't have to be awkward."

"It will only be awkward if you keep mentioning it."

She had a point. He closed the door, but he couldn't help smiling as he tossed his keys in the air and caught them. He had someone to help plan the wedding of the century.

If anyone asked, that's how he would explain his sudden good mood and willingness to hang out with a single woman. A beautiful, single woman.

Chapter Seven

Friday morning Katie bounded down the stairs of the Shaw home. She could smell breakfast, and from the aroma drifting her way it included bacon. Gwen was still getting ready. The two of them were sharing a room while Gwen was in Jasper Gulch.

Sandy smiled as Katie entered the kitchen. "You're up and cheerful this morning. It helps to have family in town, doesn't it?"

Katie poured herself a cup of coffee. "It really does. Especially since this isn't my wedding and I'd rather my sister pick her own bridal bouquet."

Sandy handed her a plate. "You're a gem, Katie Archer."

"No, I'm just used to—" She stopped herself and managed another smile. "I'm sorry."

Sandy placed a hand on her shoulder. "I have an older sister. Now, let's get you some breakfast.

I heard you're going to be filling in for our wedding coordinator."

"Word travels fast in a small town! I thought that was just a stereotype." Katie took a few slices of bacon and a spoon of scrambled eggs. Rather than going to the table, she set the plate on the counter. Sandy handed her a fork.

"Not a stereotype." Sandy went back to the stove. "In a small town we don't have a lot to talk about. We don't get out often. So when something unusual happens, word travels fast."

"I don't think my helping is that unusual," Katie said as she took another bite of bacon.

"Oh, I think folks around here will see things differently, Katie. You've been in town just over a week and you already feel like part of the community. You're pitching in to help. And we've all heard how well you handled Marci the other day. Cord—"

Sandy stopped and smiled a little sheepishly. Katie understood. The housekeeper was loyal to her family, the Shaws.

"You don't have to finish." But Katie really did wonder what Sandy had been about to say.

Gwen entered the room, all smiles. "Something smells wonderful."

"Help yourself." Sandy pointed to the stack of plates on the counter. "Would you like coffee, Miss Archer?"

"Please." Gwen grabbed a plate as Sandy filled a cup. She then turned her focused attention on her sister. "Aren't we going to sit and talk?"

Katie swallowed a bite of bacon and nodded. "Of course."

So they sat in the dining room, which hadn't been Katie's intention. She would have preferred the table in the warm, homey kitchen with Sandy. It had only been a week, but she'd already developed a routine at the Shaw ranch. She was usually up earlier than the other guests, which meant having Sandy, sometimes Nadine Shaw and the kitchen to herself.

Faith Shaw was usually up but had already eaten and gone to the barn. A couple of mornings Katie had wandered out to watch what ranch life was all about. She'd seen steers loaded to take to auction, immunizations given and other things she'd never thought to see. She'd witnessed and experienced Montana ranch life.

"How are Mom and Dad doing?" She finished the last of her eggs and refilled her coffee from the carafe that had been left on the table.

"They're a little worried, to be honest." Gwen always got to the point. No small talk about how their parents were, or about the weather or any of the other small details that made them a family.

"Worried? About the wedding?"

"No, about you."

Katie choked on coffee. After sucking in a deep breath, she stared at her sister and of course Gwen was serious. “Why would they worry about me?”

“Well.” Gwen looked around, motioning with her hands. “You seem to have taken to life in Jasper Gulch. I asked you to stay and make sure things were being planned and taken care of. You’re great with all the little details. I didn’t expect to find you ensconced in the family. When I got here yesterday you were nowhere to be found and the only person with any idea of your location was Faith Shaw and she didn’t seem to be forthcoming with details.”

Katie fought the mouth-gaping look of a guppy and hopefully managed to look as if she wasn’t totally taken by surprise. “You asked me to stay, Gwen. It isn’t my wedding…”

“You’re my sister, the best person to stand in for me.”

Of course she was. Katie knew where she fit in the Archer family. She was good at taking care of the little details for the rest of the family. She didn’t have a life of her own, they thought, so why couldn’t she be the one who took care of everything from house-sitting, running errands and now, planning weddings?

“Gwen, I am here for you. If I’m going to be here, I’m going to enjoy myself. I like the Shaws.

I'm enjoying Jasper Gulch and I'm also helping with the wedding. There's no reason for concern."

"We're a little afraid you'll do something crazy like quit your job."

Katie focused on her coffee, on sipping the hot brew and gathering her thoughts as she dealt with traces of anger. She'd never been irresponsible. But she'd also never been Gwen. And that summed up the trouble with Katie.

The trouble with Katie. She'd heard her parents say it, usually as they discussed her, and with her present. The trouble with Katie is that she doesn't take life seriously. The trouble with Katie is that she doesn't know what she wants to do with her life. The trouble with Katie…

Is that she wasn't enough.

She had never fought back. She had never told them she didn't have to be them, or be Gwen, to be happy. She was happy with her life. She was a good person. That good person had finally taken as much as she could from her family. She stood, picking up her cup and plate. "Gwen, I have to go."

"Why? Where are you going?"

"Why? Because if I stay here I'll say something mean, something I can't take back. I don't want to do that because I love you. Where am I going? I don't really know because I hadn't planned on doing anything today that didn't include you, my sister. But now, I just want to be as far away from you as possible."

"Wait, you have to—"

Katie stopped at the door. "No, Gwen, I don't."

She took her dishes to the kitchen. Sandy gave her a sympathetic look and then a light hug. "I think Faith is heading to town to pick up something from the hardware store. If you hurry, you can catch up with her."

Katie nodded and with tears stinging her eyes she grabbed her purse and hurried from the house. She was running down the front steps, wiping her eyes when she hit a solid wall coming up the steps. Strong hands gripped her arms and she looked into blue eyes. Of course, if a day could get worse, hers would. She sniffled and tried to sidestep, peering past him to search for Faith.

"I'm sorry, I was trying to catch up with Faith."

"Because you always run from the house in tears looking for my sister?"

"I'm not crying." She blinked fast and gave him a hopeful smile.

"I have sisters. I know tears when I see them."

"I have a sister, too. And as much as I love her, I'd rather not spend the day with her."

"Is there anything I can do?"

His hands were still on her arms, holding her steady, and what she really wanted to do was nod and tell him she could really use a hug. A hug would be the most amazing thing in the world. As if he knew, he pulled her close and she couldn't help it, she melted into his embrace.

"Thank you," she whispered into his neck.

"I slay dragons on weekends, if the need should arise."

She laughed a little, still being held and not minding. "I might need your services."

"So, now that you have your sense of humor back, do you want to tell me what's going on? And I think you're too late. Faith left a few minutes ago."

"What's wrong?" How could she sum up a life of not meeting expectations? "Nothing I can't handle. But I would like to talk to you about that building you have for rent."

"Wouldn't you like to take a look at it first?"

"Yes, I would."

"Okay, how about right now? I have to get some work done in town, but I have about an hour before I meet with a few people on the committee that is searching for answers into the time capsule."

"That would be great. I can always find a ride home later. And if you give me the list for the wedding, I'll see what I can get done."

"I happen to have that list in my truck. I will gladly hand it over to you."

They were almost to his truck when the front

door of the house opened and Gwen came flying out. "Wait, Katie, where are you going?"

"To town to get some work done. I meant to tell you, but I got distracted."

"Katie, I didn't mean—" Gwen stopped and sighed a little. "Okay, I guess I did. And I shouldn't have. You deserve better."

Katie glanced from her sister to Cord Shaw. He shrugged and gave her a look that said it was up to her. Up to her if she wanted to involve her sister in her plan, her dreams. Up to her if she wanted Gwen to know how involved she was with this wedding.

"You can go with us if you want."

Gwen smiled her most open smile. It was that smile that stunned people, the smile that charmed. "I'd love to go with you. Let me get my jacket."

Katie had once thought forgiving so easily made her a doormat. Somewhere along the way, she had realized that wasn't the case at all. She'd always taken her own path. She'd stood her ground when it came to college, her job, her life. She'd maybe taken a little more from her family than she should have, but forgiving didn't hurt. It hurt more to stay angry with her family, to hold on to the hurt. She remembered times that she had tried and she'd been miserable.

"You're a nice person," Cord said, opening

the truck door for her. "I hope she realizes how blessed she is."

"I think sometimes she does."

Ten minutes later they were driving down Shaw Boulevard toward Main Street. In the backseat, Gwen leaned forward. "Where exactly are we going?"

"There's a building in town I want to look at. And I have a list of things to check for the wedding." Katie glanced back at her sister. "We can have lunch together."

Gwen grimaced just the slightest bit. "That will be good. What is the building for? Won't the entire wedding and reception be at the fairgrounds?"

"Yes," was Katie's answer. Why give up too much?

Cord parked in front of the city hall. He opened the briefcase on the seat next to him and pulled out a key. He handed it to her and then a list. "Have at it. I know you'll make it all come together."

"You know you'll owe me."

"Yes, I do know that," he said with a wink.

Her cheeks heated and she stumbled over what she should say. Especially knowing that this man was so clearly off-limits. He could be a friend. Friendship was easy. It didn't hurt. It was all he wanted from her. If she remembered that, everything should work out and no one would get hurt. It was all fun and games until Katie lost her heart. She smiled ruefully at her own humor and then managed a smile for him.

Gwen was out of the truck and waiting on the sidewalk, her back conveniently turned. Her focus was on the window of city hall.

"She isn't so bad." Cord leaned toward Katie. "She thinks we need time alone."

"That's sweet of her." Time alone was a big mistake. "But I'm happy with friendship. It's less complicated." Safer.

"You won't get an argument from me," he admitted with a sheepish grin. "I've been engaged twice. Two times jilted almost at the altar."

"Okay, since we're sharing stories. I thought a man might be falling in love with me, but he just thought of me as a little sister. And then he married my best friend and I was his best woman, for lack of a better word."

"We all have scars, Katie. Some a little deeper, some a little more painful, but the scars are there. We're patched up, put back together, we heal and we forgive."

"But this, Cord—" she motioned between the two of them "—this can't happen."

"I know," he agreed. He pulled back, reaching for his door. "I want you to know, I'm not that guy."

"That guy?"

With his hand still on the door, he explained, "I'm not chasing women. I'm not looking for temporary relationships. People depend on me and I won't let those people down."

Marci and Lulu. She nodded because she understood. But it didn't really explain what had been happening between them. The big elephant in the truck with them. Chemistry? Just chemistry.

"I know. And I can't think about a relationship with someone whom I might know for only a few weeks. It's the equivalent of a summer romance in high school. The kind where the girl goes home from the beach vacation, cries for months, eats raw cookie dough and falls apart every time she hears his name. In the past year, I made a commitment not to date because it hurts too much to go from relationship to relationship with no intention of forever."

"Intentional dating?" He supplied the word.

"Yes, intentional. I'm not going to date just to date."

"I respect that. And now we know exactly where we stand."

"Yes, now we know." So she should feel better. Right? "I'll check back in with you in an hour or two. And you have my cell number if you have to leave?"

They met on the sidewalk, several feet between them. "Yes, I'll call."

She watched him walk away and then she joined her sister. Gwen gave her a curious look. "Is that why you're so willing to stay in Jasper Gulch? Not that I blame you."

Katie walked up the sidewalk to the empty store that she wanted to claim as her own. "I'm here because you asked me to stay for you and because I have vacation time."

"Right." Gwen grinned, leaning against the window as Katie jiggled the key in the lock and then opened the door. "What's this building for?"

Katie walked through the door into the small shop. Large windows faced the street. The floor had fairly new beige carpet. The walls were white but could easily be textured and painted a warm color. Potential. She turned slowly, visualizing it the way she knew it could be. In her mind she saw evening attire, casual wear, a section of Julie's wool sweaters and scarves, whatever else she might want to put in a retail venue.

"Katie?"

"I've always wanted my own store. A boutique with everything from casual to evening wear. I could carry handcrafted jewelry, maybe locally designed. Jasper Gulch has the citizens who would want a store like that and there wouldn't be any local competition."

"You would open a store here? How? Where would you live? This is exactly what we were all worried about. I could hear in your voice that you're getting attached to this town."

Where would she live? That was the question Katie stopped with. The rest of what Gwen said, well, it didn't really need a response.

She walked to the back of the store and through a door into the stockroom. There she knew she would find a door that led to stairs and the apartment above the shop. Hannah Douglas, soon to be Harcourt after she married Brody Harcourt, lived above one of the stores in town. She and her twins. She smiled, remembering those twins when she'd seen them at church. Their mother had her hands full. At least she now had someone to help carry the load.

Sometimes people found what they were looking for. Sometimes God had an unlikely plan to bring joy from mourning.

A bell jangled before she could go up the stairs. She hurried back to the store area just as Lilibeth Shoemaker walked in, looking around as if she'd never been inside the building.

"Lilibeth, can I help you?"

Lilibeth shifted her purse and nodded, looking less sure of herself than Katie thought was typical for the teen. "Yes, I'm here to see if there is anything I can do. You know, to help with the wedding. And, well, if you really are going to turn this into a store, I'd really like to work for you."

Katie blinked a few times. Word really did get around fast in a small town. "I don't have any firm plans, Lilibeth, but if you'd like to help with the wedding, maybe you could be at the fairgrounds tomorrow at two o'clock."

"That would be great. Well, I know you're busy. But thank you."

That's how a person became part of a community. She waved as Lilibeth left and then she had to face her sister and admit that she loved Jasper Gulch.

"You're not coming home, are you?" Gwen looked around the shop, her eyes somber.

"I hadn't really planned on staying. Even this morning when I thought I'd come and look at this building, it hadn't been a real plan. But, Gwen, I want this. I know it isn't an amazing plan. In comparison to your life, it is still small and it won't save lives, but—"

Gwen stopped her with a hand held up. "Excuse me?"

"You're going to deliver babies and save lives. I'm not you, Gwen. I'm not brilliant. I'm not beautiful. I'm Katie and the trouble with being Katie is that she isn't Gwen."

Gwen's mouth opened and she gasped. "You can't be serious."

"Of course I am."

"Katie, you're beautiful and funny and smart. You make people feel comfortable. Everyone loves you."

"Oh, Gwen, I wish that was the case. But I've been in your shadow my whole life. At school the teachers always expected me to be you. Our parents expected me to be you. I just want to be me. Maybe I need to be me somewhere other than Missoula. You know how sometimes a tree can't grow because the bigger tree is blocking the sun?"

"Oh, Katie." Gwen's eyes swam with tears. "I'm not the bigger tree."

"Yes, Gwen, you are. But I love you and it's okay. Maybe this is God's way of getting me where I need to be."

"God?" Gwen shook her head a little. "I'm sorry, what?"

"Faith, Gwen. Maybe that's what I've needed all my life, to have faith. And maybe I needed to see that we aren't in competition. God created us both and He has a plan for us both. A separate plan. And I've been so busy wanting your life, your dreams, that I haven't really focused on mine. I don't want to miss out on what God has planned for my life."

"I'm going to try to wrap my mind around this. And, Katie, I'm sorry for making you feel less than amazing. Because you are amazing."

Katie hugged her sister. "Thank you."

"Thank you?"

Katie hugged her sister a little tighter. "I needed you to understand because as much as I wanted a little of the sunshine, I love being your sister."

"I love you, too." Gwen backed out of her embrace and they both wiped at damp eyes. "So, we should go find your handsome cowboy? Because if you don't rope him, someone will."

"Rope him? Really, Gwen?" Katie shook her head. "I'm not trying to catch Cord Shaw."

"I think you need to reconsider."

They left the building, locking it behind them. As Katie turned toward city hall, she caught sight of a woman walking on the other side of the street. Lulu Jenson.

Cord glanced out the window of city hall. It was nearly time for lunch. He expected Katie and her sister to show up anytime. And he wanted to let Katie know that the committee had taken her thoughts on the capsule to heart. They were charged with finding it, but Olivia had already done a lot of digging on what might have been in the capsule. So far she'd found nothing.

A movement up the street caught his attention. He walked out the door when he realized it was Katie, Gwen and Lulu. Katie had an arm around

Lulu. They were obviously heading toward city hall and him.

As they approached, he heard bits and pieces of a conversation. The most telling was that Lulu wasn't sure where she'd parked her car and that someone should call her daughter because maybe she moved it. His heart ached, really ached as he listened.

Katie met his gaze and shook her head. There were tears in her brilliant green eyes and a look of sympathy so deep it moved him. He walked forward, brushing a hand down her arm before reaching for Lulu.

"Cord?"

"Lulu, it's a pretty day for a walk, isn't it?" He moved next to her when Gwen stepped back. "What are you doing in town?"

She shook her head and her eyes filled with tears. "I don't know, Cord. I really don't."

A police car drove up Main Street and pulled in, parallel to the curb. Deputy Cal Calloway stepped out, tugging down the brim of his hat as he walked toward them.

"Cal?"

"Got a call from Lulu's nurse, Pamela Gibbs. She was at the store with Lulu." He nodded in Lulu's direction and smiled. "Hey, Lulu, how are you?"

She smiled and Cord now recognized that look

on her face. She didn't know Cal, but she was going to pretend she did. "I'm just fine. It's a pretty day for a walk."

Cal motioned Cord forward. As he stepped away, Gwen took his place next to Lulu. He heard her questioning the older woman in a gentle tone. Of course, she was a doctor. He'd forgotten that detail.

"Cal?" Cord walked with Cal, putting distance between himself and the ladies.

"This is the second time in two weeks, Cord."

"I know, Cal. I know."

"Winter's coming on and if she does this in the cold…"

"I understand. I'm just not sure what to do. How do I take her away from Marci?"

The two stopped at the end of the sidewalk. Cars traveled slowly down Main Street, people rubbernecking to see what Cord and Cal were up to. Word would get around pretty quickly. He shook his head, worrying already about what Marci would hear.

"Figure something out, Cord. I won't write a report this time, but you know that if this continues, the courts could take control of the situation."

"I have medical power of attorney. Lulu doesn't have a lot of family. There's a brother in California and a niece in Arizona."

"You're probably better for her than the people

living a thousand miles away. But that doesn't make it any easier. We had to put my granddad in a home when his dementia got to this point. Hardest thing in the world, Cord. My mom cried for weeks because she hated leaving him there. But she knew he was safer because there were people constantly watching him. Some people can stay at home. But when it gets to this point, Cord, where they're wandering off and getting lost, it isn't good."

"I know. I was just hoping the medication would help her hold on a little longer."

"Yeah, it can. It didn't work with my granddad."

He glanced back, watching as Gwen hugged Lulu and spoke close to her ear. Lulu was crying, holding on to Katie's arm. Lulu's nurse, Pamela Gibbs, had spotted them and was running down the sidewalk. Cord pulled off his hat and ran a hand through his hair.

"Life doesn't always go the way we expect it to, does it?"

Cal placed a hand on his shoulder, shaking his head as he did. "Never that I've noticed."

"I'll make a decision, Cal. I just want to see if we can get her through the holidays. At least through Thanksgiving."

"Cord, if she has to go into assisted living you can still bring her home for holidays."

"Thanks, Cal."

"Anytime. You call if you need anything. And my gramps is in that place close to Ennis. It's a good facility. We checked a lot of state websites, looked at different reports and inspections."

"I'll keep that in mind."

Cal headed back to his car and Cord walked down the sidewalk where the group of women had turned into a herd. Lulu had a community of people who would support her and she had him. The two of them had been thrown together, raising a little girl who had needed them both. But Marci really needed Lulu.

Katie met him a few feet from the others. She touched his arm and the look in her green eyes was soft with sympathy. He shrugged because at the moment he didn't know what to say. Lulu stood a short distance away, her eyes darting from the group of people surrounding her to him. He swept off his hat and brushed a hand through his hair before replacing it. He was Lulu's medical power of attorney. Whether he wanted it or not, this was his life. He'd been distracted over the past few weeks and he'd failed to really pay attention to her worsening condition. Man, he hated this moment. He didn't want to have to face what he would have to do in the coming weeks and how it would change lives.

He shouldn't have allowed himself to get distracted.

"Cord?" Katie's voice edged into his troubled thoughts and he smiled at her, wishing he'd met her at another time in his life, a time that could have been easier.

He managed a smile, as if none of those thoughts had gone through his mind. "Sorry, lost it for a minute. I'm going to have to make a decision."

She nodded and then her sister approached, cautious, smiling. "Cord, I'm really sorry. I'm not sure of the relationships here, but Katie told me about Marci. I know this isn't going to be easy for you."

"How did it get this bad this fast?" He shot a look in Lulu's direction. She was talking to Rosemary from the grocery store. Rosemary must have followed Pamela Gibbs when they spotted Lulu and Cal's police car.

"It probably didn't happen this fast. She's close to seventy, correct?" Gwen asked, and waited for him to nod. "It's probably been happening but she hid it. Without a spouse to notice, it can happen this way. She was in her environment, doing her daily duties, sometimes forgetting or getting confused, and sometimes pretending she remembered."

"I've noticed that lately, now that I know what I'm seeing."

"Exactly, once we realize what we're seeing we notice more."

He looked at Katie, wondering what about that statement made him think of her. He couldn't focus on her, not now. Not with Lulu needing his help. Not with the possibility that Marci would soon need his undivided attention.

With this happening, it was too easy to remember Susan and the note she'd left, that she wanted their marriage to be about them, without extra people. Meaning Marci and Lulu. But Marci and Lulu would always be a part of his life. No matter who else came and went, those two mattered to him. Had to matter.

He had to make decisions for the two people who relied on him. "We should eat lunch and talk."

He walked up to Lulu, taking her by the hand and telling her they would work something out. He glanced in Katie's direction, including her in the invitation. He knew it wasn't exactly what she had bargained for when she stayed in Jasper Gulch to help with a wedding.

Chapter Eight

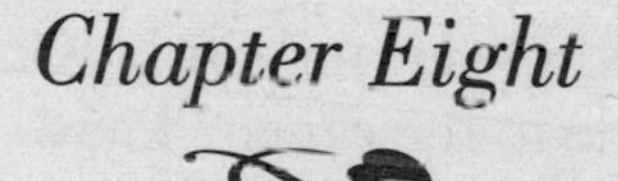

On any other day Katie would have enjoyed lunch at Great Gulch Grub. The hometown-diner atmosphere where people knew one another and stopped to talk appealed to her. Today, though, sitting with Gwen on one side, Pamela on the other and Cord and Lulu opposite, lunch was a difficult affair.

All through the meal, Lulu had tried to tell them that she would be fine. And then she cried and said she wouldn't be fine and she knew that. She knew she needed more care than Pamela could give her. She knew it was time to discuss long-term care.

So they did discuss it. Cord reached for Lulu's hand and told her they would work this out, together. He wouldn't let her down. For now, she should go home and spend time with Marci.

They walked out of the diner, an unlikely

group. Cord's sister Faith came up the sidewalk as they were heading across the street to their cars. She stopped them with a wave of her hand.

"Hey, I'm heading home." Faith smiled at the group and then at her brother. "Do you need anything?"

Katie pulled Gwen forward. "Could you give my sister a ride to the ranch? I have a few people I need to talk to, loose ends to tie up for the wedding. She won't want to be dragged around for the next couple of hours."

"I don't mind spending time with you," Gwen assured her.

"You don't have to. I have no idea how long this will take. And if Jeffrey does get away from his practice and is able to get here, you'll want to be where he can find you."

Gwen's face glowed with happiness and Katie stomped down the twinge of envy that surfaced. For her sister she would be happy. She wanted Gwen to have the perfect wedding. She wanted her to have every good thing.

"You're right," she said, and then Gwen cast a cautious look at Cord and left Katie wondering what that look meant. "You go and have a good time."

Katie pressed a light kiss on her sister's cheek. "Thank you for today. I mean that."

"I'm glad we talked, Katie. It's important for

me to know how you feel. And important for you to know how much I love you. You're my sister. I wouldn't want anything to come between us. And you're not in my shadow. If only you could see yourself through my eyes. Through the eyes of other people. You shine."

The conversation ended with another quick hug. Pamela Gibbs had left with Lulu while Katie had been talking to Gwen. Now it was Katie and Cord again, just the two of them. She didn't know how to process the strange mix of emotions that swept over her as he smiled and indicated they should cross the street.

"Let's start with Annette Lakey at the Cutting Edge Salon. Have you met her?" Cord took her arm as they crossed the street. The one car coming down Main Street slowed to let them pass.

"I spoke to her the other day. She's going to try to arrange stylists and manicurists for the morning before the wedding and day of, for women who want special hairstyles or want their makeup done."

"Then let's see what she's found out."

They walked through the door of the salon. Katie looked around the little shop, pleased with what she saw. And she really liked Annette with her dark hair streaked with color. She was pretty and confident. Annette was marrying the local veterinarian, Tony Valdez, whose office was just next door. Romance found through a stray dog. Perfect, in Katie's opinion.

"Hey, you two!" Annette was busy rolling curlers into the hair of an older woman who was reading a housekeeping magazine that appeared to be a decade old.

"We thought we'd stop in to see if you'd found some help for the wedding," Cord said.

Annette rolled another length of gray hair in a curler. "I have, actually. A few gals I know that work in Ennis are going to come in. I'll have them here Friday for styles and Saturday to fix hair for the wedding. I'm hoping for five of us. And I have some girls from the beauty school over at Ennis who are coming with their instructor to do mani-pedis on Friday. If it's okay, they'll set up shop at the fairgrounds, maybe in the festival hall? If you have an email list for all the brides, could you let them know the arrangements and give them my number for appointments? The manicures will be done from ten Friday morning until we're done. I'll also need to know who wants their hair fixed the day of the wedding so I can arrange times."

"That sounds great," Katie interjected. "And I'd like to make an appointment for next week. Just for a trim."

Annette eyed her red hair and nodded. "You're a natural girl, I like that. Do you highlight, or are the lighter streaks natural?"

"Natural. And no perm. I rarely even blow-dry."

"I'll put you down for next Thursday then."

A sharp bark from the back cut into their conversation, and Cord laughed a little. "I thought you said you wouldn't keep that stray?"

Annette turned a little pink. "Naming Stormy was my first mistake. And Tony loves that dog. Stop teasing me. I've seen you pick up a stray cat on the side of the road."

Cord cleared his throat and Katie smiled, knowing he was wanting to get back on track. "We won't mention that. Annette, I have to ask you something."

"Uh-oh." Annette shot him a look. "Is this bad news?"

"Not at all. I'm just wondering about you and Tony, your wedding..."

The woman getting her hair done chuckled and Annette frowned first at the reflection in the mirror and then at Cord.

"I already told you, I'm getting married in December. I thought you had fifty couples."

"We do but there's always the chance someone will back out."

Katie immediately thought of the bridezilla, Andrea. She knew Cord must be thinking of her, too.

"I really don't want to do a fifty-couple wedding, Cord. Not even for you, honey."

"You're sure?"

"As sure as any woman can be. And that's pretty sure. Why don't you find yourself a bride between now and then? Isn't it about time you got yourself leg shackled, as you men like to call it?"

"I've never called it that, Annette, and I don't think Tony thinks that way, either."

At that, Annette smiled a huge smile and looked all fluttery. "No, he doesn't. But since you're so worried about having enough couples…"

"I think we'll just go now," Cord said as he reached for Katie's arm to steer her toward the door. As they exited, they heard Annette's bright laugh and her customer saying something that made her laugh even louder.

As they walked out the door, they met Hannah Douglas coming down the sidewalk, a twin on each side of her. The toddlers held tight to her hands and walked on unsteady little legs. Katie stepped back, smiling at Hannah Douglas. Katie had met Hannah and her twins, Corey and Chrissy, at church on Wednesday.

"Hey, Hannah, how are you doing?" Cord asked as the mom and two little ones stopped on the sidewalk. The little boy plunked down and his tiny fingers went for a blade of grass growing out of a crack in the sidewalk. Hannah swept him up, settling him on a hip while still holding her daughter's hand.

"Hannah, do you think your babies could be in the wedding?" Katie asked.

Hannah laughed at the question. "I think not."

"No?"

Hannah kissed her son's pudgy cheek and he giggled. "No one wants to arm these two with flowers or anything else that might be used as a weapon."

Cord laughed. "It could be fun."

"No, not fun for some poor bride wanting a beautiful wedding. Count these two out. I don't think I could take it."

"Do you know of any little girls that would be suitable? I think about a half dozen. The company that is lending the vintage wedding dresses also has children's attire. I was talking to the owner and she has pretty dresses of different sizes and colors." Katie reached for one of the twins, lifting the little girl in her arms to give Hannah a break.

"I can make up a list of girls in the preschool class at church," Hannah offered. "I'll have their parents contact Cord, or give you all the numbers. Are you helping with the wedding, Katie?"

"Yes, since the coordinator had to back out, I've been helping Cord."

Hannah looked at Cord, her eyes widening just a hint. "That's great. I know he isn't fond of weddings."

"You would think after a while a guy would

lose that distinction." Cord reached for the little girl trying to get away from Katie.

"I know and I'm sorry." Hannah took the girl from him. "I'm going to see if these two will take a nap. Make the wedding beautiful, Katie. I'm not doing this again."

"I'll do my best."

They left Hannah to her twin dynamos and headed back in the direction of city hall and Cord's truck. First they stopped in at the bakery, heard about the final arrangements for the wedding cakes and the caterer that had been consigned for the event.

"It had to be good, growing up here." Katie spoke as they crossed Shaw Boulevard. "How does it feel to have a street named after your family?"

Cord chuckled. "Like a weight. In the city, you have some anonymity. In Jasper Gulch, everyone knows whose kid you are. If you pull a caper, everyone knows your folks. If you get jilted at the altar, everyone knows the story."

"I suppose that's true. But it feels as if you always have a friend in Jasper Gulch."

He brushed his shoulder into hers. "With sentiments like that, my dad will have you making the next town brochure for the chamber of commerce. Which I would welcome, because I'm tired of being the technological go-to guy. I can see it now—Jasper Gulch, where you always have a friend."

"See, that makes me want to move here next week."

"Will you?" He opened the truck door for her.

"I'm thinking about it."

As Cord climbed behind the wheel, he glanced at his watch. "I have to pick Marci up at school. I think it's time she and I had a hard talk about Lulu. Do you mind riding along or should I take you to the ranch first?"

"I don't mind riding along. But I understand if you'd rather do this alone."

He nodded and started the truck. For a minute, he sat there, staring out the window. Distracted, he brushed a hand against his cheek and then he turned, smiling, but it was a dim version of the real thing. "It's been just the three of us for a long time, but I think Marci might like it if you're there. I just don't want her to get any ideas."

Ideas about Cord and Katie. She got that. Little girls built fairy tales around romance and weddings. "I understand."

A few minutes later, they were pulling up at the school. She waited and let Cord go in alone. There were reasons. She needed a minute alone. But Marci needed to see that it was Cord who would be the constant in her life.

* * *

Cord signed Marci out, getting permission for him to drive her rather than her riding the bus. He was already listed as one of her guardians with the school. He'd been this person in her life for a long time. But she'd always had Lulu. That was the change that would rock her eleven-year-old world.

"Why are you picking me up?" she asked as she swung her backpack over her shoulder. He took it from her and was surprised at how heavy the thing was.

"What do you have in here, rocks?"

She laughed a little, but he heard her nervousness in the sound. "Yeah, and bricks. So, don't change the subject."

"Your grammy had a rough day," he explained as they walked across the parking lot.

"She's been having a lot of rough days. It scares me."

Honesty time. "It scares us all, Marci."

"I don't want her to die."

"She isn't dying."

"But it's the same as. She isn't going to know me. She isn't going to cook fried chicken or make peanut butter cookies."

He wrapped an arm around her thin shoulders. "No, she isn't."

"I don't want her to change." The matter-of-fact

tone took him by surprise. She didn't cry. She didn't scream. She was Marci. Life had dealt her some rough blows from an early age. This was yet another.

He felt kind of like a sissy when he thought about everything she'd gone through compared to his own problems. The kid was a rock. He had to work on being as strong as an eleven-year-old girl. Pretty eye-opening.

"We'll get through this, Marci."

"You have to go to church with me, Cord." She shot him a look. Wise beyond her years and strong.

"I know."

"And you have to learn to cook."

"I cook."

She spotted Katie in the truck. "And I'm going to need a mom."

"You're pushing it." He bumped into her a little.

And then she sniffled. "I'm not going to cry."

"Sometimes you will. We'll probably both cry. But that's okay."

She nodded and headed for the truck, climbing in the front instead of the back. He watched her clamber over Katie, and Katie helped her get settled in the seat. Cord took a deep breath and headed for the driver's side of the truck to face whatever was coming at him.

He tried not to think about Susan walking out

on him because he was a package deal and part of the package was Marci and Lulu.

When he got in, the conversation wasn't at all what he expected.

"Someone said they're going to tear the Beaver Creek bridge down," Marci said as she snapped her seat belt in place. "I told them they don't know anything."

"They aren't tearing the bridge down," Cord responded. "We want to repair it and open that road back up."

"They said the town is better off without it."

"I disagree." Cord shot her a look as he pulled out on the road. "Why were sixth graders discussing the bridge?"

"Because we're talking about politics and stuff and about how votes change things. Did you vote on the bridge?"

"No." He laughed a little as he answered. She might be president someday. "We didn't vote. But we have a committee and we're making the decision that is best for the community."

"That's what I said. I thought I was going to have to hurt Jimmy Hayworth."

"Don't hurt anyone."

She shrugged. "I'm hungry."

She was the quick-change conversationalist. "We can stop at the store and see if Rosemary has any chicken strips under the warmer."

The preteen in her came out and she rolled her eyes. "Because I love things under warming lights. Do you realize that warm light is just helping salmonella to grow? It's like a petri dish."

Katie laughed, covering the sound with her hand. She glanced out the window and he couldn't make eye contact with her. Man, she was beautiful, though. He wondered if she had any clue how her eyes lit up with humor, how her mouth was perfect and kissable.

Marci elbowed him. He glanced down and her eyes had narrowed and she was giving him a look. If he had to guess, that was a "don't be obvious" look.

Eyes back on the road. He drove down Massey, stopped at the stop sign and turned on Shaw Boulevard and headed for the store and the salmonella strips that would take the edge off Marci's hunger until dinner.

The Massey sign reminded him that he still had one or two Masseys, maybe a dozen, to try to contact for the festival. It would sure help the town if he could get at least one of them to show up. Or at least, that was his dad's opinion. Maybe the Masseys thought that after all of this time it didn't really matter if they came back?

He parked in front of the store and next to him, Marci let out a squeal. It didn't take him long to see the reason. Joe Banks was sitting on the bench out front and he had a box of kittens. Great.

He could already see the need and want in Marci's eyes as she hurried out the passenger side. He thought Katie looked almost as done in by the sight of that box of kittens. Furry bits of fluff and trouble. That's what he saw in that box. He saw messes. He saw ripped curtains, clawed furniture and a tormented dog.

Marci had a long-haired gray kitten in her arms. He walked up, scratching his head and wondering how in the world he'd get out of this one. Especially when Marci passed that kitten to Katie and grabbed one that had long hair but looked more Siamese.

"Joe," he greeted the old farmer who had recently retired and bought a house in town.

"Cord." Joe grinned a knowing grin. *Gotcha,* that grin said.

"Marci, you know—"

She turned sad brown eyes on him. "We could keep it in the barn at your place."

Right, he knew how that would work out. "You know you're not going to leave that kitten in the barn."

Her eyes lit up. "You mean I can keep it in the house?"

His house. It hit him that very soon she would be residing in his home. And she knew it. They both knew the change was coming. He wasn't a swearing man, but if he had been, there would have been words to say at that moment. Not about a kitten but about the unfairness of life.

He'd been wrestling God for eleven years about that very thing. He'd missed more church than he'd attended. He'd been angry. He'd wanted a different outcome.

This time he was a little older. A lot older. He sighed and nodded. "You can have a kitten. The litter box and feeding it are your job."

She looked between the two kittens. He could see that she'd thought about pushing it and asking for two. In the end, she picked the gray, snuggled it close and told him she wasn't really hungry. They did have to run inside and get kitty litter and food.

As they got back in the truck, his phone rang. The way things were going, he knew it couldn't be good. He glanced at the caller ID and saw his dad's name.

"Dad."

"Cord."

Okay, they were already at a standoff.

"Can I help you?"

His dad sighed long and low, a sure sign. "Why do you have the Time Capsule Committee searching for something that doesn't exist?"

"What, do you mean the time capsule that is missing? As far as I knew, it existed."

"I mean, why do you have them searching for something that might have been in there, like it's a big scavenger hunt? Livvie gave you a list of what was in there. Old newspapers and the like."

"Dad, this is just a thought, but it could be there was something in there that someone wanted to hide. Maybe the Masseys beat us to it. Did you ever think of that? Maybe an article in one of those newspapers?"

"Hogwash," his dad mumbled. "You're just stirring up talk. You know that the people on that committee aren't going to keep quiet. I was in the feed store ordering grain and they were discussing it in there. Who had something to hide? What could embarrass a family? Of course, they looked at me because I'm a Shaw."

"Dad, that wasn't my intention and I think you know that. You've been a bear with a thorn in his paw for months. I'm not sure what's up with you, but what I've done isn't a problem." He paused for moment to think. "Unless the Shaws have something to hide."

"No!" his dad snarled. "No, we don't have anything to hide."

The phone went dead. Cord shook his head and tossed the thing on the dash. "Well, that went well."

"Maybe I should have stayed out of this?" Katie suggested.

"No. I think this has more to do with him and my mother than anything we've suggested about the time capsule. I can't remember them ever having a difference of opinion that lasted more than a day. I'm not even sure they're having one now. I think they're just not communicating and he's a little off because of it."

They pulled into the driveway of Lulu's house. Marci looked at the house and then at him. Her kitten was held to her cheek.

"It's going to be okay," Cord offered. He hugged her and she hugged the cat. "I'm always going to be here."

"I know. I just don't want Grammy to go away." Marci leaned toward Katie. "I've been singing the song with her. She even plays it on the piano."

"That's good, Marci. I know she loves making that memory with you."

Marci nodded, and as Cord got out, she followed. Katie shook her head. "I'll wait here. There shouldn't always be a stranger in the middle of everything."

He walked Marci to the door. Lulu was waiting. She smiled when she saw the kitten. Cord's attention shifted to the truck and to a woman who should never be compared to anyone else.

He was glad she'd stayed in Jasper Gulch, glad

she had found her way into his life. For Marci's sake, he was glad she was there.

Yes, it was a lot easier to accept her for the sake of a child than to admit to himself that he liked Katie Archer for more reasons than just the simple fact that she'd made things easier for Marci.

Chapter Nine

The festival hall of the fairgrounds was crowded with women. The men were meeting in town at city hall with a company that would supply reproduction suits from the same era as the dresses. Katie stood in the sea of lace, silk, satin and tulle. Someone had shoved a bridesmaid's dress into her hands to try on. She didn't have time. Not yet. Nor did she have the inclination.

The dresses were beautiful. She walked among the women in creations of silk, satin, velvet and lace. The dresses came in all shades of white. Many were the layered-lace creations from the early 1900s. A few were empire-waisted with long flowing skirts. And a couple of ladies had picked gowns from the Roaring Twenties.

Gwen stood on a makeshift pedestal, their great-grandmother's dress hanging loosely from her petite frame. The dress was softest silk in warm white. The sleeves hugged the arms, rather than the puffy sleeves of some styles. The skirt fell to the ground with casual grace. Katie wanted to cry as the seamstress discussed the alterations to make the dress fit.

She walked away, nearly bumping into Julie Shaw, who was wearing Elaine Shaw's gown of soft, draping lace. The antiqued color fit Julie's auburn hair and autumn coloring.

"What do you think? Veil or no veil?" Julie asked as she turned in the dress that barely fell to her ankles.

"No veil. I think some of the women are doing decorated headbands. You could even attach some lace to the headband to let it hang down in the back."

Julie clapped her hands together and smiled. "Perfect. And did you see the flower girls Hannah rounded up from church? They look like little cherubs in their pretty dresses."

"I did see them." Katie looked at the group of girls in their white lace gowns. "They look like trouble in waiting."

"Yes, they do." Julie got the words out and then she was pulled away by Nadine, who was enjoying marrying off her first daughter. She was talking about hair and something borrowed being Julie's grandmother's pearls.

Katie moved on because it hurt to watch that

mother-daughter moment. Olivia Franklin, the other local bride, was trying on a borrowed dress. Tiny, with blond hair, she looked gorgeous in the lace dress that came just above her ankles. Olivia had the look of a woman in love. And who could blame her? Jack McGuire, her soon-to-be husband, was as kind as he was gorgeous. The one-time high school sweethearts had been reunited after years apart. Being around all these happy couples, even Katie was starting to believe in real love.

The photographer had Olivia against the backdrop they were using for photos. He handed her an enlarged picture and had her hold it in front of her as he snapped pictures. Katie hoped the idea was as cute in reality as it had been in her mind.

The next bride up was Hannah Douglas, today free from her twins. She held a picture of a serene young woman in the same dress she was wearing. The velvet dress draped her in winter white and she looked absolutely stunning.

All around her, brides wore shining smiles and hopeful expressions. Of course they did. They were all planning new lives with the men they loved. And Katie was still carrying the autumn-brown gown that her sister had picked for her. It was a silky affair that hung to midcalf. It was beautiful, really.

As she circled the crowd, watching to make

sure everything was going as planned, Lilibeth approached her, all smiles because she'd been able to help pick dresses for some of the women.

"This is amazing. I wish I had someone to marry so I could take part." Lilibeth said it with that certain romantic smile of a young woman who knew someday her fairy tale would happen.

"It is going to be quite an event." But Katie almost agreed with the beautician, Annette, who wanted her own ceremony in the quaint Mountainview Church.

"Robin is trying to match pictures with women. I think since she only has thirty she's going to recycle so some women will hold the same picture," Lilibeth offered.

"That will work. It isn't so much about who is in the vintage portrait, more that we're tying the two generations together. After all, shouldn't marriage today mean the same as it did one hundred years ago?"

"What a nice thought." Lilibeth sighed as she agreed.

Katie smiled at the younger woman. She genuinely liked Lilibeth. "I'm going to see if I can help Robin."

She headed toward the photographer. Robin was pushing through the photographs she'd found for them to use in their wedding photos, and to hang in the reception hall during the wedding reception. Julie was up for her picture. As she moved to the spot the photographer indicated, Robin pulled out a candid photo of a young woman in front of a new automobile. New for that time period. Katie knew it was a photo of Elaine Shaw, great-great-grandmother of Julie, Cord, Adam, Austin and Faith. She'd been a beautiful woman.

Robin handed the photo over, her heart in her eyes. Katie wondered if perhaps Robin wished she, too, was getting married in this ceremony. But like Katie, Robin was a temporary resident in Jasper Gulch.

After Julie's picture was taken, Gwen stepped up. She had a photograph of their great-grandmother in the same dress. Katie managed a bright smile for her sister because Gwen deserved this moment of happiness. She deserved this wedding and a beautiful marriage to the man she loved. And Katie knew how to cover her emotions. It's what she did. She wouldn't let Gwen see her cry, or see even a hint of her sadness.

She wanted her sister to be happy.

Katie walked outside, needing fresh air. As she walked to the corner of the building, footsteps crunched in the gravel behind her. She started to turn, but a voice spoke close to her ear.

"You are amazing."

She smiled at that gruff voice and the scent of

mountains, pine and fresh air that seemed a part of the man. "I'm not amazing. I'm out here because I'm jealous of my sister."

She turned to face Cord. "She's wearing the dress I've wanted to wear since I was a little girl. I used to sneak into my mom's closet just to look at that dress."

There, she'd actually said it. She'd admitted it to this man. A stranger, really. But maybe that's what made it okay to tell her secret. In a matter of weeks she'd be gone and this would all be a part of the past.

Cord leaned close, his forehead against hers. "I repeat, you're amazing. Gwen has to know how blessed she is to have you. I know that I'm glad that God put you here in Jasper Gulch."

"Because what would you have done without me?" She smiled as she said it, but smiling was the last thing she wanted to do. Cord was glad she'd dropped into his life when he needed her to help him through a difficult time. She wanted more.

She hadn't realized until that moment just how much more she wanted.

Cord felt a flash of some emotion as he looked at the woman standing in front of him trying to smile, trying to make everything okay.

"You're right. I couldn't have done it without

you. But I'm glad you're here because I would have missed not knowing you."

She groaned and closed her eyes, leaning to rest her head against his shoulder. "Could you stop saying the right thing? Just once say something ridiculous and insensitive?"

He found his arms going around her. "I think I've done that more than once. I'm trying to be your hero, so maybe you could give me a break."

She stood on tiptoe and kissed him. He didn't move when their lips first touched. And then he pulled her close and welcomed her lips against his. Everything within him told him to be careful. With her heart and his.

A month ago he never would have expected this moment or the way he felt with her in his arms. Hopeful? As if he might want to take another chance? As if God had known he would need this woman in his life. For a season? For this short time?

He kissed her lightly one last time and pulled back. He didn't say anything. If he did, it would be wrong.

Screams from inside the hall pulled him back to the present and into the real world. Someone shouted, "Come back!"

Another person shouted, "Stop! Just talk about it."

Cord turned as the door of the festival hall

flew open, banging against the outside wall. The bridezilla's groom rushed from the building. What in the world was a man doing in there? The men were at city hall trying on suits. Ace, the groom, was wearing jeans and a flannel shirt. He shook his head as he turned to face Andrea.

Andrea in her lace wedding dress chased after him. "You are not going to do this to me. You come back here now! I'm warning you."

The groom stopped and Cord wondered if he was going to give in to her demands. Instead, he shook his head and held up a hand to stop her pursuit. "I'm not marrying you, Andrea."

"What does that mean? Of course we're getting married. We sent out invitations. We're having a reception when we get home. We've already received gifts."

"I'm not marrying you until you realize we're a couple. You have to learn to share your life with someone. I'm not going to marry you and be your puppet. I'm not your servant. I'm the man who wants to marry you. I've been over there trying on suits for our wedding and you've been sending me texts telling me I'd better do this the way you want."

"It's my wedding!"

"It's *our* wedding." The unhappy groom shook his head and took a step, a promising step toward Andrea.

Cord wondered if he should try to help. Somehow he thought Ace had this handled. He hoped, pretty selfishly, that the other guy had it handled.

Ace had given up moving forward and was stepping away from his bride. "It should be our wedding, Andrea. I'm leaving. If you decide to make me a part of our life, then you let me know."

"I will," she pleaded. "I'll do whatever you want, but you can't embarrass me this way."

"Once again, it's about you. I will not get married at this ceremony."

He turned and walked away. Andrea screamed a feral scream and ran back into the festival hall, leaving the door wide open. Cord looked at Ace getting in the smart car and then back at the building where there was no sight of Andrea. Next to him he heard Katie gasp and then laugh a nervous little laugh.

"Marriage is a beautiful thing," Cord said as things seemed to calm down. "And now we're down to forty-nine couples."

"What will you do?"

He shrugged, taking off his hat to brush a hand through his hair. "I don't have a clue. We've marketed this to the media as a centennial celebration, a wedding with one hundred people."

"So you find another couple. Surely you can find someone in the area who would like to get married?"

"Yes, that should be easy to do in two weeks."

"Annette and Dr. Tony?"

"I can try again. Maybe if I make it about saving the community?"

"I think that won't work. She is pretty set on what she wants." Katie peeked into the building where Andrea was ripping off her veil and rushing through the room. "Maybe a couple wanting to get married who hasn't considered this ceremony?"

"I can't think of anyone." Cord pushed the door closed. "This is not great. Maybe I should have tried to talk him into staying."

"You would do that to him?"

"No, I couldn't. Not in good conscience."

Katie cast another cautious look at the door. "I should go in."

"I don't envy you."

She shuddered a little. "I really don't want to."

He gave her another easy kiss on the cheek. "I have to get back to the men, who are far less emotional. But while I'm here, I'm going to impose again."

"I'm not marrying you."

He flinched. "Ouch. At least you're not waiting until we're about to get married to tell me. I wasn't asking you to marry me. I was going to ask if you would go with me this week. I'm taking Lulu to a facility between here and Ennis. I want her to see it, to feel good about it. And I want Marci to know what we're planning. I'll take her out of school to go."

"Of course I'll go."

Because she never left a friend stranded. That's who she was. He'd known she would say yes. And now that she had, it felt wrong.

He reached for her arm as she started to walk away. "I shouldn't do this to you."

She faced him again, her green eyes asking questions, her cheeks pink from the cool October air. "What?"

"I'm taking advantage. You always do what people need you to do. It's who you are. You're the go-to girl for all your friends. You're here for your sister because she asked. Now you're there for me, for Marci, for Lulu, because I asked."

"I want to do this for you." She caught her lip between her teeth. "Cord, I'm not a victim being used by everyone. I'm going with you because I genuinely like Lulu and Marci. I want to be there for them."

"Thank you, that does mean a lot." His attention drifted from her to the car leaving the parking area, the ex-groom's, from the way the car spun out and gravel flew.

"You'll find a fiftieth couple."

"I hope you're right. I never thought this would be easy to pull off. I definitely didn't count on the headaches it would cause."

"Two more weeks."

Yes, two more weeks. He wondered if she would really move to Jasper Gulch. How would it be if she stayed and they saw each other on Sundays at church or at the café during lunch hour?

"Yes," he agreed. "Two more weeks. We can do this. I'll call and let you know when I'm taking Lulu."

"Won't you be at church tomorrow?"

He hadn't thought about it, but, "Yes, I'll be there."

It had been a long time since church had been a given in his life. He thought maybe he'd taken faith for granted. It was what the Shaw family did, they went to church. They prayed. They trusted God and they gave their tithes. He'd avoided church for several years, but he felt as if he was going back knowing more about himself, more about his own faith.

He watched as Katie hurried back inside the festival hall. He could hear the women inside, talking and laughing as they tried on dresses. He thought about Katie in the dress her sister would be wearing down the aisle and how she wanted to be the one who wore that dress someday.

It was the wedding. It was getting under his skin, making him think about things he'd been determined not to think about again. A woman in a white dress, a wedding ring, lifting a veil to see a bride's face and a kiss that meant forever.

All the things he'd almost had. Twice.

The wedding would be over in two weeks and he'd go back to his old life. The life before this centennial celebration started taking over their town, their lives. But he wouldn't really go back to who he was before.

Chapter Ten

The Shaw ranch was huge. Thousands of acres of Montana grassland and mountains. Katie stood next to the barn and watched as Adam and Austin Shaw moved cattle to acreage closer to the main house. They'd been branding and tagging calves, giving shots. She'd gone out with them yesterday, just to watch the process. Cord had been there, the older brother, the brother who gave too many orders and got under the skin of his younger siblings. She'd enjoyed watching and then enjoyed the hot lunch Nadine drove out in her truck.

She walked Nadine's poodle, Ranger, and the dog pulled on the leash. He wanted to keep moving, keep sniffing and investigating. The morning walks had become Katie's way of helping out. She enjoyed the walks with Ranger, keeping the little dog out of trouble, and Nadine enjoyed the extra time it gave her to take care of book work, which was her duty on the Shaw ranch.

With Gwen gone again, Katie needed to keep busy, to feel as if she wasn't just wasting time here. There were moments when she thought she should go home. There were more moments when she wondered if she would ever want to leave Jasper Gulch.

"Come on, Ranger, time to go inside." She didn't have to force the issue. The sound of a truck had Ranger's attention and the dog turned and started back to the house, pulling on the leash to go home. It was Cord's truck.

"Are you really that excited to see him?" Katie asked. In response, Ranger yapped a few times. "Fine, he is nice and I'm usually glad to see him, too. At least you can't tell."

The dog led her down the driveway, back to the house that looked stark in the middle of this valley with few trees and the blowing grass turning brown. The mountains in the distance looked gray this morning, gray but capped with white snow. Winter would be here soon.

Cord had stepped out of his truck. Lulu and Marci were still inside. Marci waved and Katie waved back. She headed in Cord's direction, but not because she had a choice. Ranger tugged on the leash, pulling with all of his eight-pound might. It turned out eight pounds of determined was actually very strong.

"Ready to go?"

She nodded and held tight to the leash. "Let me put him in the house and grab my purse."

"We'll wait in the truck. If I go inside, I might never get away. I think Mom is doing some end-of-year stuff and she always has questions."

Katie headed for the house, pulling the reluctant poodle. She finally picked the dog up because it was easier than fighting him on the leash.

She'd learned a lot about ranching in her short stay at the Shaw ranch. She knew that the business side of taking care of cattle was huge. It was a family corporation with taxes, investments, expenses and salaries. There were also big losses, Nadine explained. An early snowstorm could do them in; so could drought, if they had to haul hay from other states.

She released Ranger, hung his leash on the door and called out to Nadine that she was leaving. A moment later, Nadine appeared in the living room, looking a little frazzled.

"You're going with Cord to take Lulu to Mountain Acres?"

"Yes."

Nadine gave her a steady look and then nodded. "It won't be an easy day."

"No, it won't."

"I'm glad you're going." Nadine walked with her to the door. "Cord has a habit of not relying on people. Katie…"

"Yes?" They stood in the doorway and Katie wanted to escape whatever Nadine Shaw might say. In the end, the older woman shook her head and told her thank you, as if that made sense.

Katie hurried out to the truck, running against the brisk wind that blew at her. Marci had the door open to the back and Katie climbed in next to her, behind Cord in the driver's seat. Lulu stared straight ahead, not responding when Katie spoke.

Marci reached for Katie's hand and held tight. She held tight on the drive to the facility, Mountain Acres. She held tight as they toured the home. They walked through the dining area, the sitting rooms and the activity room. They visited a room with two beds, two recliners, two televisions. Lulu walked to the window and looked out at the brown grass of the garden area. The sky beyond was laced with gray clouds, the blue just barely peeking through.

Lulu turned and smiled at them. "Why did you say I'm here?"

Cord stepped next to her at the window. "Lulu, do you remember what we talked about? That you need more care?"

Lulu nodded and her hand rested on his arm. “Is this the home you told me about?”

“Yes, it is.”

“And you’re leaving me here? Where will Marci sleep?”

He sighed and his shoulders stooped and Katie wanted to make it all go away for him, for Marci and for Lulu. Marci held tight to her hand, and Katie watched as she flicked away tears.

“Marci will sleep at my house. You gave me custody.”

“Oh, yes, that’s right.” Lulu turned to face them, smiling at her granddaughter. “You know this is a very nice place.”

Marci nodded.

“You’ll come and visit me and we’ll sing.”

Marci ran to her grandmother, wrapping thin arms around the only parent she remembered. “‘In the Sweet By and By,’” the child mumbled against her grandmother’s waist.

“‘We shall rest on the beautiful shore.’ I won’t forget, Marci.”

“I know.”

“We’ll sing it together every time you visit.”

Marci nodded, but she didn’t release her grandmother.

Cord walked away, leaving the two alone to come to terms with their near future. Katie followed him out of the room and the administrator walked with them.

"We'll help her get on a schedule and keep her routine. That's important for Alzheimer's patients," she explained. "When they know their surroundings and things are kept the same, they seem to do better. We'll do our best to make her happy and of course you can visit at any time."

Cord brushed a hand through his hair; his face was etched with the pain of making this decision. Katie placed a hand on his shoulder, wishing she could do more. He covered that hand with his and then he raised it to his mouth and kissed her palm. His eyes were closed and he slowly shook his head.

"I wish I didn't have to be the one doing this to them."

"I know." She leaned in close, holding his hands. "But you're the one who cares the most, which means you'll make the best decision."

"I keep thinking that if she stays at home, we can help her. We can look after her. We could hire someone to live in full-time."

"Cord, you know..."

"I know."

Behind them were footsteps. Katie glanced toward the room and saw Lulu with Marci. They were holding hands and the nurse was walking with them. Marci burst into tears and ran at Cord, wrapping her arms around his waist and not letting go.

Lulu touched her granddaughter's head, stroking the blond hair. "I'm not going home, Cord. I'm staying."

"Lulu, we're just here to look at this place."

"No, we're here for me to stay. I planned it this way. I could go home and in a week or two you would need to bring me back. But I can't keep doing this, worrying that I've forgotten to turn off the stove, worrying that I haven't fed Marci. Sometimes I worry that I don't know her. That isn't good for either of us."

"Lulu, we can work this out." Cord held on to Marci and with his eyes implored the older woman, who seemed to have already made a decision.

Katie reached for his arm as he stepped forward, taking Marci with him.

"Cord, I'm staying. I have my purse and it has what I need for a day or two. Someone can bring the rest. But Marci needs a home that is safe and someone looking out for her. For the past few weeks she's been taking care of me. That isn't fair for a little girl. So I want you all to give me a hug and promise you'll visit."

"We'll visit, Lulu," Cord said.

Lulu reached for her granddaughter. "Marci,

honey. Please sing with me one more time before you go."

Marci flew to her grandmother's arms and sobbed as they sang together, "'There's a land that is fairer than day and by faith we can see it afar…'"

Lulu stroked Marci's hair and as they sang she pulled away.

Marci fell into Katie's arms and Katie held her close for a minute before leading her out of the nursing home while Cord waited with Lulu. If she'd known when she came to Jasper Gulch that this would be her journey, she thought. And then she took it back. She would still have come. She would still want to hold this child and be a friend to that man.

It was late afternoon when Cord pulled his truck into the driveway of Lulu's little house on the edge of Jasper Gulch. He sat there for a minute, the truck running, Katie in the passenger-side seat with Marci leaning against her. He had to turn off the engine and go inside that house with no Lulu to greet them. He had to pack a bag of her belongings and he had to pack what Marci would need for a few days. Until they could move, well, whatever they would be moving. He had the power of attorney to dispose of the house and property. He guessed he'd keep it for Marci. For someday.

"We should go in," Katie finally said.

He nodded and turned the key in the ignition. "Man, this stinks."

"Yes, it does. But you'll get through it."

He agreed, he would. He glanced at the sleeping form of the girl he'd promised to always watch out for. Now he would be raising her. He didn't know if either of them was ready for what was ahead of them. But he knew they'd give it their best.

"Yeah, we'll get through it." He opened the door. Marci woke up, groggy and brushing hair back from her face. "We're home."

She nodded, grabbed her jacket and slid to the door. Katie climbed out on her side and followed them up the sidewalk to the front door. They entered the quiet house with furniture from a few decades earlier. Worn but comfortable, Lulu always said. She loved this house with the big windows, the outdated colors and the kitchen with new appliances he'd bought her the previous Christmas. She'd always wanted one of those stoves without burners, she'd said. He'd bought her one. And the stainless-steel fridge that matched.

Marci stepped into the house, looking around as if she expected Lulu to greet them, wiping her hands on her apron and telling some story about

Joe down the street or that ornery Rusty Zidek. Rusty had been a friend of Lulu's dad. History. This town had it.

"You need to pack some clothes, Marci."

He wished he'd framed the request in a different way. The second the words left his mouth he knew he should have given her more time. Katie shot him a lethal look and he shrugged.

"Why don't you show me your room?" Katie requested and Marci took her up on it. The two of them headed down the hall to Marci's bedroom.

Cord stood at the window wishing he had another choice for this day, another way it could end. Katie returned to the living room a few minutes later. He saw her reflection next to him in the window.

"Cord, she's pretty wiped out from the emotion. Why don't we let her stay here tonight. I know you have a lot going on, but I don't. I'm the person who was dumped here by my sister, left for your family to feed and shelter. I could stay with her. It will give us time to go through her stuff and time for her to adjust."

Cord brushed a hand over his face and wished he could think like a woman. It wasn't happening, though. He could, however, admit when a woman had a good idea. "That sounds like a good plan. I can run over to the café and get dinner."

"I think that will work."

He glanced at the clock on the wall. "I'll head that way now. I know what Marci wants, what about you?"

"I'll have the taco salad."

He nodded and hit the door before he could do what he really wanted to do, take Katie in his arms and thank her for being there for them. For him.

When Cord pulled up to the café it wasn't crowded. Of course, it wasn't quite dinnertime. He walked in, removing his hat as he did. The waitress, Mert, stood behind the counter. She raised her head and gave him a serious look.

"I heard about Lulu."

"How in the world do you people find out this stuff before I can even make it back to town?"

"Well, Beulah, my neighbor, has a granddaughter who has a friend who works at Mountain Acres."

He groaned.

"And that's how it works," Mert said with a light tone but no smile. "You know, Cord, I didn't see this coming for Lulu. I guess I've seen her slipping a little. For the past year or so she'd forget things. But we're all getting older and we're all forgetful from time to time."

"I know, Mert. I was the same. I think the only ones who really saw were Lulu and Marci."

"How's the little munchkin?"

“Not good.”

“No, I don’t reckon she is. Let me fix you up her favorite and I’ll throw in the chocolate pie. On me.”

“You don’t have to do that, Mert.”

“Well, of course I do. Cord, this town really cares about that kid. She’s kind of belonged to all of us and we’re all still here for her. And for you.”

“Thanks, I’m going to need all the help I can get.”

She patted his arm as she headed for the kitchen. “No, you’ll do okay with her. Besides that, you’ve got that pretty Katie Archer to help you out.”

When he got back to Lulu’s, that pretty Katie Archer was sitting on the couch. Marci was sprawled out sound asleep on the other end with her kitten curled up next to her. Katie looked up as he walked through the door. He held up the bags of food and carried them to the kitchen. Katie joined him.

“How is she?” He asked the question that he already knew the answer to.

“She’s exhausted, and sleep will probably do her a lot of good. We went through her room and packed a suitcase of clothes. We also packed some pictures from her walls, her stuffed animals and a few games. Cord, this has been a long year for her. I think as sad as she is, there is also a little part of her that is relieved."

"Relieved?"

"Because now everyone knows. Lulu would forget things, important things. She would forget groceries and how to turn on the stove. She even forgot how to cook certain foods."

"And Marci didn't tell me?" His mind went back, really trying to think about Lulu for the last year. How long had Lulu known the truth about her condition and kept it from him?

"Marci was worried, Cord. And she was protecting Lulu. Her grandmother told her not to tell you because you'd worry."

"I should have noticed."

"They were good at hiding it."

She walked up behind him as he put the food out on the counter. He set out the disposable containers and then he turned, pulling her into his arms. She whispered against his cheek that she was sorry and those words undid the resolve of the past few years, to do this on his own. He wasn't a superhero, just a man who'd had enough of being let down.

He wrapped his arms around her, holding her tight. She felt good there, close to him, holding him. He wanted to bury his hands in her hair, claim her lips, never let go. The thought took him by surprise. It was the wrong time for this, for a relationship. He seemed to have a knack for bad timing.

He would like to think that maybe God had been preparing him for this moment and Katie. All the mistakes, the heartache, were leading up to making him the right man for the right woman.

And maybe it was just years of loneliness making him irrational.

He hadn't even realized he was lonely until Katie. He did know that when she left, he'd be lonelier than ever before.

Chapter Eleven

When Gwen and Jeffrey returned that week they brought Katie her car. She slid behind the wheel of her Jeep, glad to have her own transportation again. After the previous day, taking Lulu to Mountain Acres, she seriously needed a drive, a way to clear her thoughts. She also needed to make a trip to Missoula. Maybe she would do that the next day. Today she was going to see the area and explore a little.

Anything to get out of the house and away from the crowds. With less than a week before the wedding, the brides and grooms had returned full force. The Shaw ranch was overrun with emotion, a few prewedding spats and too much lace.

She drove through town, making her way to the gas station before heading out River Road toward the Beaver Creek bridge. Or what was left of the bridge. She also wanted to see how things were progressing at the museum. When she'd first come to town, the siding had been going up. It would be interesting to see how far it had progressed in the weeks since. Three weeks. It was hard to believe she'd been here that long. And then, it was hard to believe she hadn't always lived in Jasper Gulch.

As she got closer, she could see the bridge that spanned the river. From a distance, a person wouldn't know that the bridge wasn't passable. Up close, one could see the disrepair. Barriers had been put up to keep people from driving or walking across.

The museum was on a piece of land just before the bridge. In front of the metal building with the faux-wood front, giving it an Old West look, stood Cord and several members of the city council, including Mayor Jackson Shaw. She noticed Rosemary Middleton from the store, always a good source of helpful advice and gossip, and several others whom she'd met but couldn't always keep their names straight.

Katie parked her car and got out, not planning to interrupt the meeting. She walked down to the bridge and watched as the water of Beaver River flowed beneath them. She tried to picture the accident that had led to the loss of Lucy Shaw. Her body had never been recovered. Katie had heard there had been a lot of rain and the river had been up, moving fast with a strong current. It was hard to believe that this meandering river could become a giant that would take a life. The road on the other side of the bridge seemed decent. She knew that if the bridge was repaired, Jasper Gulch would grow. There would be tourists from Yellowstone. There might be fly fishermen.

There would be growth that would change the small town. And growth that would keep it alive. She understood both sides of the issue.

She walked along the river for a short distance. The day was warm, almost sixty degrees Fahrenheit. The sun was bright. In the distance, blue skies were an exquisite backdrop for snow-capped mountains. She looked up, turning slowly to take in the beauty of this wild countryside. She stopped and squinted. In the distance, she saw a herd of deer. They were small and moved close together.

"Beautiful, isn't it?" Jackson Shaw came up to stand next to her.

"Yes, it is."

"Cord said you might be staying in the area, renting that little store of his."

"I'm thinking about it." She didn't want to say too much, but tomorrow she planned on giving notice to her boss in Missoula. Even if she didn't decide to take the store in Jasper Gulch, this trip had convinced her to take a step in a new direction.

"It would be good for Jasper Gulch to have a clothing store. The ladies would probably like to buy something other than work jeans at the feed store."

She smiled up at the older Shaw. "Yes, sir."

"Well, I guess I'll head home. Nadine has some chores for me around the house. I try to tell her that's why we have sons, but she doesn't always agree." He smiled and tugged down on the brim of his hat. "You have a good day, Miss Archer."

After a few minutes, she followed the path back to the museum. Cord had walked away from the group of council members. He waved and headed toward her. Katie stopped, waiting for him. He was in his element here, a rancher with confidence, knowing who he was and where he belonged in the world. She'd always pretended to have confidence but she had never felt it, not with that assurance.

"Want a tour?"

She nodded. "That would be nice."

"Watch your step. We still have concrete work to do out here. The inside is shaping up. We're putting up the interior walls."

"So it should be done soon?"

He opened the front door for her and they walked in. "Not until we get more money. We've done what we could and we'll have money from the wedding but not a lot. In the next week or so, we'll probably bring construction to a standstill. The fund for rebuilding the bridge isn't even close to enough for that project. It seems like we're hitting a wall and I have to wonder if we should just let it all go."

"Give up?" She smiled at him.

"Well, when said that way, I guess not."

They walked around the large, open room. She knew that Olivia Franklin had been putting together a great collection for the museum. There would be photographs, letters from the past, articles left behind by settlers who first came to Jasper Gulch. It would be a shame if the collection was never given a home.

"My dad didn't bother you down at the river, did he?"

Katie looked up at the unexpected question. "No, of course not. We talked about your building and if I would stay in Jasper Gulch."

"And will you? You haven't really been definite."

"I'm praying. I know I'm making a change, but I'm still not sure what exactly that change will be. I came here for a wedding and fell in love." At his look she continued, "With Jasper Gulch. But does that mean I'm supposed to stay? It's a big decision."

"Yes, it is. I was afraid he was pushing you to walk down the aisle with me. He's worried that ninety-eight brides and grooms is not a record-breaking number. No one is going to show up for that wedding, and the couples participating were promised this amazing wedding that broke records."

"I don't think any of them are really worried about breaking records. They love the dresses, the history and the uniqueness of the event."

"I hope you're right. I wouldn't be surprised if he isn't on his way to church."

"To pray?"

Cord's hand touched her back and he guided her out of the building and back into the bright afternoon sunshine. "No, to see why Pastor Ethan Johnson hasn't asked Faith to marry him."

"Are they dating?" Now she was really confused.

"No, but my dad would like it if they were."

They both laughed as Cord walked her to the Jeep. She pulled the keys out of her pocket and stood there, unsure of what she should say. "I'm going to head back to the ranch. Tomorrow I'm going to Missoula for the day. There are things I need to take care of there."

"Are there any details I need to take care of, with the wedding?"

"No, I think we're actually all set. There will, of course, be last-minute things later in the week."

She climbed behind the wheel of the Jeep. "How is Marci?"

"She's good. She wants me to invite you out for dinner. She has decided I'm not a terrible cook."

"She's a great kid, Cord."

"I know she is. After school we're going to visit Lulu."

"Give them both a hug for me." Katie started the Jeep, ready to drive away. Cord had once been the man she thought was safe. He wasn't looking for someone. He was easygoing. A friend. Now he was the biggest entanglement of her life. She loved his dimple, the scar above his eye, the way his hair felt beneath her hands.

She loved when he held her. She loved him. She shook off the thought. She loved who he was, that was an easier statement, easier to deal with. She loved the way he treated his family, the way he took care of Marci and Lulu. The way he treated her like a friend who mattered. Not a friend good for a laugh or a quick call when he was lonely, but a real friend.

No! This couldn't happen. Not now, not with this man. She wouldn't fall back into the pattern of loving men who didn't feel the same.

"Katie?"

She blinked a few times and smiled what she hoped was a convincing smile, one that didn't give away the realization that had just dawned on her. He had taken up space in her heart in a way no other man ever had. He got her. Had anyone ever gotten her before?

"Yes, I'm fine. Sorry. I was thinking about how much this town means to me." It wasn't really a lie.

"Will we see you later?"

She shook her head. "No, I think I'll head on to Missoula for the night."

"Okay. Be safe. While you're gone I'll try to round up a new bride and groom before my dad tries to force someone to the altar."

She backed out of the parking lot and she was proud of herself for not begging him to love her back. If she was going to stay in Jasper Gulch, she had to accept that Cord was a friend, a good friend, but he wasn't a man looking for a woman to walk down the aisle with him. At least not for real.

Cord left the museum and headed for the Cutting Edge again. As he walked through the door, Annette shot him a look, the same kind of look a woman gives a badger in her chicken coop. He was reduced to being vermin.

"I told you no. I think I've told you no more than once."

"I know, Annette, but you've met my dad. He's

pretty determined to have fifty couples and you're the only other couple I know of."

"Maybe you should find your own bride."

"If I had a woman on the hook, don't you think I'd try?"

She leaned over the counter and smacked her gum at him. Then she smiled. "And here I thought you were sweet on that pretty gal from Missoula, Katie Archer. I'm doing her hair in a couple of days. Do you want me to put in a good word for you?"

"Please don't help me, Annette."

"Well, you can't seem to get a bride on your own."

"Oh, I can get them, remember? I've had two. It's the 'getting them to the altar' part that I've had trouble with in the past. I'm not trying to prove that practice makes perfect."

She patted his hand that rested on the counter. "Well, at least you can laugh about it now. You're a good man, Cord, and you need a good woman to help you raise Marci."

"I think Marci and I are good on our own. I hired a lady from Ennis as a live-in housekeeper, that's the only woman I need in my life right now. She's sixty, doesn't want to get married and she understands that Marci is important. To be honest..." He paused, guessing it must be the beauty shop effect—why else would he be telling Annette these things? "It wouldn't be fair to any woman who came into my life to have to come in knowing that I'm devoted to making sure this kid and her grandmother are taken care of. It wouldn't be fair to Marci if I got sidetracked."

"That's a load of hooey, Cord. That's fear talking. You can care about more than one person at a time. And the right woman won't be a distraction, she'll love that kid right alongside you. Susan wasn't the right woman."

He shrugged off the Susan comment. "Are you sure I can't talk you...?"

She shook her head. "Don't ask me again, Cord. I'm not getting married at that ceremony."

"I won't ask again."

"Promise? You know I do things my own way." She patted her neon-streaked hair.

"I promise."

She held out a hand, her pinkie finger extended. "Pinkie promise?"

"What good does a pinkie do?" He laughed as he hooked his pinkie with hers. "Other than make me feel like I'm on the playground again?"

"It made you smile, that's what it did."

He released her pinkie and let out a sigh. "I'll smile a lot more when this wedding is over. And thank you for not making me spit in my hand and shake on it."

She laughed at that, and he thought what a

fortunate guy Tony Valdez was. "I considered it, but figured I'd pushed you far enough. You give Marci a hug for me, Cord."

He tipped the brim of his hat and headed for the door. "I will."

As he crossed the street to Great Gulch Grub, Rusty Zidek caught up with him. "Where's the fire?"

Cord glanced at the older man. "Is there a fire, Rusty?"

Rusty laughed at that. "Stop being so serious, Cord. Take it from an old man, life has more good times than bad."

"I'm sorry, Rusty. I've just had this wedding up to my neck. I can't find a couple to replace the one we lost. I hope an epidemic of couples breaking up doesn't happen. Wouldn't *that* be good publicity?"

Rusty followed him through the doors of the café. "Well, from what I see these days on the TV, bad publicity seems to bring business. Look at some of these singers acting out the way they do. Instead of ignoring them, which is what you ought to do with naughty children, people rush out and buy their records."

"They aren't records anymore, Rusty," Cord teased as they took a seat together.

"Yeah, I guess everything is all newfangled and digital. I was over at the library the other day and set me up an email account. I don't know what I'll do with it, but I have one."

"You can email family," Cord offered.

"Yeah, I guess. Or I could pick up the phone or even write them a letter."

Cord had to ask, "How did we get on this conversation?"

Mert headed their way, a smile on her face and an order pad in her hand.

Rusty laughed at Cord and turned over the coffee cup for Mert to fill it up. "Well, I reckon you started it."

"No, I don't think so. I think I mentioned trying to find a couple for the wedding."

"And that's how we got here."

Mert cleared her throat. Cord smiled up at her. She had the ability to look like a warden, but then her eyes would sparkle with humor and she'd smile. "You two going to order or waste my time?"

"We'll order," Cord answered as he picked up a menu.

Rusty took a sip of his coffee and ordered a burger. "Any word on the time capsule?"

"None at all. Not a trace. Not a clue." Cord looked the menu over, not that he needed to. "Burger for me, too."

Mert shook her head and walked away.

"It'll turn up," Rusty said. No one could accuse the older man of getting sidetracked.

Cord raised his eyebrows. "Really, you think?"

"Yeah, these things have a way of working themselves out."

"Rusty, what's in that time capsule?"

Rusty toyed with his coffee cup. "You think an old man like me knows something like that?"

"Well, if anyone would…"

"You think it would be me?" Rusty looked up, meeting his gaze head-on. "Cord, that was a long time ago. Livvie done gave you a list of what was in there."

"Yes, she did. And I guess it was a long time ago."

"And you have other things to worry about, like how to keep that pretty redhead in town."

Cord shook his head and wished he'd done anything other than come to Great Gulch Grub today. "I'm not sure why you'd say that."

"Well, I guess I say it because if I was fifty years younger…"

Cord laughed, "Fifty years?"

A smile broke across Rusty's aged face and he tugged on his gray mustache. "Well, maybe about seventy years younger."

"I think you'd have a chance, even at fifty years younger."

"I do have a way with the ladies. Been thinking

about courting a certain someone." He glanced up at Mert as she returned to refill their coffee.

"Don't be looking at me, you old codger."

They all laughed and Cord, for a few minutes at least, was able to forget the bridge, the museum and the wedding. He was able to forget that Marci and Lulu were depending on him. He almost forgot about green eyes the color of a spring meadow. But then he saw her drive down Main Street in her old Jeep and the man sitting across from him kicked his shin.

"That's what I'm talking about." Rusty inclined his head toward the window. "If I was a young single man."

"Which you aren't."

"You're testy today," Rusty pointed out.

Cord drew in a breath and reached for the ice water Mert had left. "I guess I am. There's a lot going on around here."

Rusty lost his smile at that. "Yes, son, there is. Something that should have drawn us all together, this celebration, has put some of us on different sides. Plus, this time capsule situation and whatever pushed someone to take it. But we haven't lost our sense of community or our faith, have we?"

"No, Rusty, we haven't. Because with everyone divided, they're still pulling together and making this happen."

"That's right. And you've got a lot going on in your personal life. That'll all work out, too."

"I know it will. The important thing is making sure Marci feels secure."

Rusty stopped for a minute as Mert placed plates of food in front of them. He poured a glob of ketchup on his burger and grinned at Cord.

"Doc says I should lay off red meat, it's gonna kill me." He chuckled as he took a big bite. After swallowing and then taking a drink of coffee, he shot Cord a look. "I guess it will eventually."

Cord shook his head, laughing a little at the idea of red meat killing a ninety-something-year-old man. "Rusty, I'm glad I ran into you today."

"That isn't what you were thinking thirty minutes ago when I first caught up with you."

Cord looked down, studying the burger on his plate. "Yeah, well, I was wrong."

"That's what I like to hear. A man who can admit when he's wrong. Don't worry, Cord, this month will be over soon. There will be about fifty 'I dos' and you'll be able to take a deep breath."

Right, at the end of the month, life would return to normal. He wanted to believe that but he knew better. Marci was talking about painting the room she'd claimed as her own. Katie was thinking about renting his store.

This was his new normal.

Chapter Twelve

On the way to church Wednesday evening, Katie ended up with Beth, the other sister-of-the-bride. As Katie had headed for her Jeep, Beth had called out, asking for a ride. Katie had waited for the woman to catch up and the two had headed out together, ahead of the rest of the crowd that had converged upon Shaw ranch.

The crowd was so large inside the house that Katie had felt somewhat claustrophobic and had spent most of the day in town making sure everything was ready for the wedding. She couldn't help feeling a sense of pride. They'd pulled it off. The flowers, the cakes, the decorations, the reception.

"You've been busy since I've been gone." Beth had left for about ten days. She lived in Billings and had a job at a bank.

"Yes, I've been helping put the wedding together." Katie turned on the road right off Shaw

Boulevard that led to the church. She'd been here long enough that she knew every road, every side street and every business. Not that there were many of them.

"Someone said you might stay?"

She didn't want to make this announcement to Beth. "There's a store in town for rent."

"That would be exciting. I couldn't imagine living in a town this size, no matter how gorgeous the ranchers who live here."

Katie didn't comment. She pulled into the church parking lot. It was dark and golden lights glowed from the windows. She had never had a church to call her own. She'd never really had a place she felt like she belonged to. But pulling into this parking lot felt a lot like coming home.

It felt good to be here.

She climbed out of the Jeep, not really meaning to ignore Beth. She had so much on her mind, so much to work through. And some things were becoming very clear. She walked with the other woman, who kept up a steady conversation about the wedding, her sister's dress, the tent and how romantic it would be with the candlelit chandeliers.

Katie made appropriate comments. And then they were inside. She slipped out of her coat and hung it on a hook in the entry. Beth followed, still talking. Katie searched and finally spotted Marci talking to Faith Shaw. When Marci saw her, she raced down the aisle, all smiles.

"I have a catalog. Cord is letting me redecorate and he said I could show you the stuff I like."

"How fun, Marci. Did you bring it with you?"

Marci shook her head. "No, it's at the house. Maybe if you come out before the wedding we can look at it."

"I'll try. But if not, I'll be by in a few days and we'll pick out some great stuff."

"Don't break the bank." A deep voice from behind her startled them both.

She spun to face Cord. "I didn't see you here."

"I was in the office with Ethan. It seems the entire town is circling, worried he'll die old and alone. I commiserated since I've been in his shoes."

"Gotcha," she replied, but what else could she say? "Did you find another couple?"

That was the wrong thing to say.

"No, not yet. Maybe we can talk after church?"

As if on cue, the recorded bells began to play, the melodious sound ringing across the valley. Everyone paused to listen.

"It would be better if we had the real bells, don't you think?" Cord asked. "I know they wouldn't play a tune, but the simple ringing of bells, calling people to church."

Faith walked up behind her brother. "Wow,

you're spiritual all of a sudden. What happened to the brother who attended church on holidays and when Mom could guilt you into coming?"

Faith glanced past her brother and smiled at Katie. The smile made assumptions, about Katie and Cord. The cornered look on Cord's face meant he had noticed, too. Because she was helping him, they were being seen as a pair. Katie needed to take a step back, from Cord, from what felt like a friendship she wouldn't want to lose. Because a man like Cord, a man wanting to stay committed to a child he was raising and her grandmother, wasn't looking for more than friendship. He needed her help and she'd been willing, but she couldn't be more. He wasn't looking for more. And she deserved more. For a couple of weeks she'd nearly brushed aside that commitment she'd made to herself last year, but the trip to Missoula had helped her remember. She didn't want to do this again. She didn't want to chase a man, hoping he'd be the right one, wanting to make him the right one.

Cord's voice pulled Katie back to her surroundings. "I never stopped believing, Faith. I just… I think we've had this conversation."

Faith arched an eyebrow and smiled. "Yes, we have. I just wondered what changed that you're suddenly here every time the doors open."

"Katie, if we can talk after church?" he asked, brushing off the comments made by his sister.

She barely nodded before he shot his sister a deadly glare and walked off, Marci on his heels.

Faith looked a little bit sorry as she led Katie to an empty seat. "I shouldn't have been so hard on him."

What did Katie say to that? She could tell Faith that three weeks didn't make Katie an expert on Cord Shaw. She could say that in a matter of days she would no longer be living at Shaw ranch and so it really wasn't, had never been, any of her business.

"We've kind of pulled you into our lives, haven't we?" Faith continued as if Katie had answered.

Katie couldn't help the turn of her lips. "Yes, just a little. Do you do this to everyone?"

"Only the people we really like. Which is you. And I'm so excited that you might stay and open a store. You are staying, aren't you?"

"I think I might." She still hadn't told anyone. Why not start with Faith. "I quit my job while I was in Missoula. So it's either here or somewhere else. I really need to slow down, though, and make sure I'm making the right decision."

"I vote for here. I hate having to drive so far away to shop for something decent to wear."

"Aren't you in Bozeman quite often, playing in

the symphony?" Katie knew that Faith was extremely talented. And perhaps not the most confident of Shaws. In some ways, she thought the two of them might be the most alike.

"Yes, but I don't enjoy shopping, and I really don't enjoy the city. I love life here in Jasper Gulch and on the ranch. So, if I could shop here and not have to trudge through the malls of Bozeman, I would be so happy."

"I understand. Well, I don't, really, because I love to shop."

They both laughed but then started moving forward. People were taking their seats. Faith reached for her hand and gave it a squeeze. "Promise me you won't hurt my brother."

Katie sat in stunned silence for a moment. "Faith…"

What did she say to that?

Faith's fair skin turned a little pink, highlighting the sprinkling of freckles across her nose. "I'm sorry, I shouldn't have said that. He's my brother and he's seen me through some hard times. I want him to be happy."

"I'm not sure…" *What to say,* she thought.

Faith let go of her hand. "You don't have to say anything. I know my brother, and I know that he's smiled and laughed more in three weeks than he has in years."

"I don't think that's because of me."

Fortunately the music started to play. At the last second Faith leaned close and said, "I do."

Those were the last words Katie wanted to hear. "I do." With all the wedding preparations, they had become too significant. She didn't want to hurt Cord. She also didn't want to be hurt. And he could hurt her. Cord put so much of himself into the people he was committed to. Did he have room in his heart or his life for a woman, for a relationship?

It shouldn't matter, she told herself. She hadn't come here looking for a man. She hadn't even planned to rent this store or move here. But moving here meant day in and day out of Cord, of talking to Cord, seeing him, hearing about him.

And someday, when he realized he could juggle a relationship and Marci, when he realized a woman could love both him and the child he cared about, where would that leave Katie? As the best friend in waiting?

Maybe she should rethink the building before her heart was broken, this time in a way that she couldn't comprehend. In the past it had been crumpled, somewhat bruised, but never really broken. Cord Shaw could truly break her heart.

Cord sat at the back of the church. When the service ended, he couldn't say he'd had any big revelations. But he had found peace. He'd been angry for a lot of years. Angry with God for what happened to Angie, Marci's mother. Angry because Susan had left him. Angry with his best friend.

Anger had nearly eaten him alive. It had kept him bottled up inside himself. But the anger was misplaced. He'd been battling people and believing he'd been wronged.

But maybe the best thing that had happened to him was Susan leaving. He'd known before she left that they weren't right together. He looked back now at what would have been nearly six years with the wrong woman. Why in the world was he mad that she'd left and spared them both that heartache?

The service ended and he met Katie coming down the aisle. She didn't see him at first. He watched her, with her red hair pulled back in its customary clip. She wore a brown sweater, a multicolored scarf, jeans and boots. When she saw him, she smiled and it wasn't so bad, to think that smile was for him and only him.

"I didn't see you," she said.

"I noticed you were in another world. How are you?"

"I'm good. I'm excited about the wedding. And excited to get it over with."

He looked around at the groups and at people leaving, "Have you seen Marci since church ended?"

"She's with Julie, telling her about her plans for her new room."

Oh, he knew. "Yes, she's going to redecorate. She wants rustic but she says she needs kid rustic."

"She *is* a preteen."

Yes, she was. "Do you have a few minutes?"

"Of course," she said, but she looked suspicious.

"It's about the wedding," he added. He believed in full disclosure.

"Ah," she said.

But she walked with him toward the exit. He spotted Julie and held up a finger. She understood and nodded.

They walked down the steps and headed up the sidewalk away from the church.

"No fiftieth couple yet?" Katie asked as they walked.

"No. I even considered having a couple renew their vows. I tried my folks, and my dad said getting married once is enough."

"I'm really sorry."

They continued to walk away from the crowds, away from the lights. The night was cold and he heard her sniffle. He wrapped an arm around her shoulders and pulled her close, causing a shift in his heart he was coming to recognize. This woman had changed everything. Her laughter, her willingness to care, it all merged to wrap him up in something he wasn't quite ready to put a name on. It was easier to call it attraction. He was definitely attracted to her.

What else could he say? He'd been engaged twice to women he thought he'd spend the rest of his life with. Women he thought he loved, and he thought they'd felt the same for him. He remembered what she'd said days ago when he told her about those engagements, that he'd dodged the bullet. Twice.

Maybe he'd dodged bullets and instead of spending his life avoiding relationships he should be thankful for the chance to someday find the right woman.

At the end of the sidewalk, they stopped. She glanced back at the church and then up at him.

"Well?" she asked, her voice hesitant.

"Katie, would you marry me on Saturday?" He smiled as he said it. "I've tried everyone. If we don't have a hundred people, the deal is off. No records are broken, the media doesn't care and the couples probably will back out."

"That was very romantic. I nearly swooned."

He saw the humor in the situation and laughed, but his laughter faded as he looked down at the woman staring up at him, lips slightly parted, jewel-colored eyes glistening in the cold.

"I could get down on one knee, if you'd like."

"Please don't, that would be embarrassing. Both the situation and you stuck there as I walk off." Her gloved hand reached for his. "I can't take vows that aren't real, Cord."

"We won't take them then," he promised as he saw an opening. "We'll walk up. When they say the vows, we won't."

"I can't lie to family and friends. I can't lie to your family."

"Katie, we'll tell our families. I'm not trying to trick anyone. I'm just trying to keep this event from falling apart and I'm out of ideas."

"I'm a last resort?" She said it in a voice that didn't waver, but he heard the sadness and that was the last thing he wanted to do to her.

"No, Katie, you're the only one I would ask. I'm not looking for a bride to walk down the aisle with me, but if I was, and since I do need—" He stopped because he was making a real mess of things.

Behind them, people were leaving the church. Cars and trucks were pulling onto the road, headlights flashing in the darkness. She shivered in her jacket and looked up at him.

"There are other women in this town, Cord.

There are people you've known your whole life. Why would you pick me?"

That was a question he'd been asking himself for a few days. Why was it that every time he thought about a couple walking down the aisle at this wedding, he pictured the two of them? Because she was there, convenient and helpful? She wouldn't expect anything other than his friendship? That wasn't fair. That put her back in the very box of willing friend that he knew she wanted to avoid. He understood her. He understood her fears, her desires. She wanted to be well and truly loved before she gave her heart because she'd given it too many times in hopes that someone would love her back.

He didn't want to be another man who hurt her.

"I trust you." His simple answer brought a smile to her lips.

"I trust you, too." She brushed her fingers across his cheek and he turned, kissing the tips of those gloved fingers. He heard her indrawn breath as his mouth stilled on her hand, and he felt a strange pleasure that she had that reaction to him. Slowly she withdrew her hand.

And then she nodded.

"You'll do it?" He would be real embarrassed if he sounded breathless.

"I'll do it. I..." She shook her head. "As much as I know better, I'll do this for you."

She started to walk off, but he reached for her hand and stopped her escape. "I understand that this is asking a lot."

Her back was to him and he wanted to wrap his arms around her and nuzzle her neck. And that was the problem. When Katie was around, his thoughts turned to holding her, to keeping her next to him. He could have told her that and made it all better. But he couldn't. As much as he trusted her as a friend, he couldn't give more. Not now, when Marci's heart was on the line, too. Marci, who was depending on him for stability, for happiness.

"Cord, let's not talk about it. I'd rather just say yes and not have this conversation about you understanding."

"But I do."

She spun so quickly she nearly lost her footing. "If you understood, you wouldn't ask me to do this."

But he did. And yet he had asked. "I'm sorry. And you're right. I shouldn't have. I'm sure there is someone else I could ask."

She pointed a finger at his chest. "But why not ask Katie, she's easy to get along with and she'll do anything to help you. Right?"

"Not exactly," he said, hoping to say at least one right thing before they parted for the evening.

Finally she spoke, softly. "Marci is waiting for you."

"Kate, I'll find someone else."

She shook her head. "My name isn't Kate."

He brushed a hand down her cheek, pushing a stray tendril of hair behind her ear. She shivered beneath his touch. "I think you're Kate. Katie is the girl you were. Kate is the woman I admire."

"So Katie is the girl who always plays the supporting actress. The best friend, sister's helper, fun to take to a party but she never gets the leading role."

The best man at the wedding. Her sister's shadow. He understood because he knew her. And he knew she was so much more than that role she'd allowed herself to fill.

"Kate, you're more than that. If this hurts because you think I'm taking advantage of our friendship, I don't want you to do it."

"I'll need a dress. And a bridesmaid. I think Marci would be good. But then Gwen will need a bridesmaid. And you'll need a best man. Maybe Adam."

"Katie," he started.

She stopped him, poking her finger into his chest. "I'm Kate. I'm a woman who is doing what she wants for a friend, not Katie who is being coerced."

"Thank you." He leaned and slowly settled his lips against hers. It was biting cold, but their lips together were warm. "Thank you," he whispered.

For so much more than agreeing to this plan.

"Is there something going on that I should know about?"

Cord raised his head and glared at his sister. "You should know that you're hard to get along with."

Julie laughed at that. "Right, well, Marci is over there wondering where the two of you will go on the honeymoon and if she gets to go with you. So you might want to take things down a notch before Ethan marches you inside and makes this official."

"We're sealing the deal," Katie offered with a smirk.

"The deal?" Julie looked from Katie to Cord.

"We're going to be the fiftieth couple," Cord offered and then waited.

Julie choked. She blinked and shook her head. And then she gasped. "You what?"

Yes, it was as good as he thought it would be. Next to him, Katie laughed and reached for his hand.

"It won't be real," Katie explained. "There has to be fifty couples and we're going to be that couple. But we won't really take the vows. We won't have a marriage license. We're stand-ins."

Julie's eyes narrowed on him, her brother. "So you're going to get married but not really mean it? As opposed to Dorie and Susan—"

He cut her off. "You know, let's just leave it at that, problem solved. Wedding saved."

"I'm not sure, but if the two of you think this is a good idea…" Julie shot a cautious look in Katie's direction and Cord followed, noticing the slightly lost look on her face that was quickly replaced by a smile. Julie started to say something else. Fortunately, she was distracted by Marci hurrying down the sidewalk in their direction.

Katie looked at him. "You have to tell Marci. She has to know because she can't think…"

That it was real. He got it.

"Are you two almost finished?" Marci asked. "I have school tomorrow."

"Yes, we're finished."

"And? What's up?" The preteen sounded way too old to his ears.

"Katie and I are going to be the fiftieth couple at the wedding Saturday."

Marci immediately squealed and started jumping up and down. Katie stopped her with a firm hand on the shoulder. "We aren't really getting married."

The bouncing stopped. "You aren't?"

Katie shook her head. "No. We're filling a place so that the wedding can go on."

"Oh, I see." To Cord, it was obvious she didn't see.

Katie smiled at the girl and then at him. "I

should go and you can explain. Tomorrow I'll get a dress."

Not the dress she'd always wanted to wear, he thought. And he knew it would hurt. He knew walking down the aisle as the best man for a man she'd thought herself in love with had hurt her. He knew walking down the aisle with him, not a bridesmaid but not a bride, would hurt. And he wondered if she could really do it.

"It'll be beautiful," he offered.

"Yes, beautiful."

And then she was gone. Marci stood in front of him, arms crossed in front of her and her mouth quirked into a disapproving line. He searched over her head for Julie, but Julie was getting into her old truck, slamming the door twice to get it to latch.

"What?" he asked.

"You're not as smart as I thought."

"What does that mean?" He hit the remote on his truck and pointed. "Get in."

"I'm going, but I'm telling you, you aren't smart."

On the way back to his place, he glanced at Marci. "What did I do wrong?"

"I think you know and if you don't, you have to figure it out on your own."

"I'm trying to figure it out."

"Right, and I'm a kid so I can't always tell you everything or you'll never get it on your own."

"Okay, fine." Was he really having this conversation? What happened to the man he'd been a month ago? The man who had it all figured out. Or maybe he didn't have it figured out and he did need an eleven-year-old to point things out to him. "Marci, Katie and I are friends. She doesn't mind helping me."

"You are a horrible judge of people. By the way, in case you miss this, I want to be adopted by you. And I'd like to be Marci Shaw."

"We're going to work on that. Can you give me a break? I did get you a kitten."

"Yeah, that's true. And I'm trying to help you get me a mom."

He choked and she reached to pat him on the back. "You had to know that was coming."

He shook his head and tried to form words, but the words didn't come. A lot of thoughts did, though. Thoughts of walking down the aisle with Katie. Thoughts of kissing a bride who wasn't really his bride.

He'd probably just made the biggest mistake of his life.

Chapter Thirteen

"Why are we going to Ennis?" Gwen sat next to Katie in the car. They'd left Jeffrey to go fly-fishing with Adam and Austin Shaw.

Katie didn't quite know how to answer her sister. She'd tried last night when she got home from church. Gwen had been in their room reading a book. Katie had settled on the bed and tried to think of a way to explain the fake marriage. It wasn't as much about not wanting to tell as it was about how much it hurt.

And it shouldn't hurt.

"Katie?"

"Kate. I'm Kate now."

Gwen studied her and then nodded. "Okay, Kate, what's up?"

"We're going to Ennis so you can help me pick a wedding dress. And then you'll have to call a friend and see if you can get a new bridesmaid. If you can't, I'm sure I can come up with one."

"Wait, back up. Let's take this one thing at a time because you're really making me a little nervous. First, a wedding dress?"

Katie blinked because she wasn't going to cry. "You know that we had one couple leave. To really make this wedding a record-breaking event, newsworthy, they need those fifty couples."

"So you're getting married just to make that fiftieth couple. Really?"

"I'm not really getting married. Cord and I…"

Gwen held up a hand to stop her. "So Cord Shaw has something to do with this, of course. And is that why I'm calling you Kate?"

She nodded and one tear did trickle down her cheek. She swiped it away. "Yes and yes. I'm doing it because I care about this town and what happens to it, Gwen. Not just for Cord or because he asked. I thought about this last night and honestly, I could have said no. It wasn't about feeling as if I have to do this to keep his friendship. I did it out of friendship, but I am also doing this for a town that feels more like home than anyplace I've ever lived."

"Okay." Gwen was silent for a long time after that.

Katie drove to Ennis and followed directions to the shop that was supplying dresses for the wedding. She parked and the two of them got out and walked up to the store.

"Are you sure you want to do this?" Gwen asked as they stepped through the door. A bell jangled and someone in the back called out that it would be a minute.

"I'm sure."

"Have you decided to stay in Jasper Gulch?"

"I've been praying about that." Katie looked at her sister with that statement that was so out of character for her, for their family. "I'm going to get the wedding over and then make the final decision. But I think I might."

"Have you told Mom and Dad?"

"About which, the wedding or staying?"

"Both."

Katie flipped through the book of dresses on the counter. "Yes. I called this morning to tell them about the wedding and my part in it. I've also told them about staying."

Gwen smiled as she stood next to her. "And they were thrilled."

"Supportive as always. They said that I'm making a big mistake, giving up a job that gave me stability and grounded me, and that this is just me being flighty."

"You aren't flighty. I know you've given this a lot of thought."

"I really have. I'm also considering a side job.

As a wedding coordinator." A job she could do anywhere. She liked that idea. She loved the idea of giving brides the wedding of their dreams. The weddings of her dreams.

"You would be amazing, Katie. Kate."

Katie smiled at her sister's attempt. "Thank you for that."

They stopped at vintage dresses and looked over the photos. "Kate, wear Eva's dress."

Eva, their great-grandmother. Katie glanced at her sister. "What?"

"You have always wanted to wear that dress. I knew that, but then I heard about this wedding and it was vintage. I took over and I took something you wanted."

Katie didn't know what to say. She paused on one dress and stared at it, not really seeing. Gwen's hand rested on her arm.

"No," Katie finally answered. "You are really getting married. I'm taking part in a faux marriage. The dress should have a real wedding, one with real vows and real love."

"The dress should be worn by someone who really loves it."

Katie had to agree, but the other obstacles blocked her from agreeing. She shook her head and then the proprietor of the store walked through swinging doors that separated the front of the store from the back. The woman, a pretty blonde named Eileen, smiled in recognition.

"Katie, what brings you in today?"

"I need a dress. For the wedding."

Eileen glanced from Katie to Gwen. "But, Gwen, didn't we take care of..."

Gwen shook her head. "Not my dress. Hers."

"You're getting married?" Eileen clasped her hands together. "At the Jasper Gulch ceremony?"

She nodded, unable to tell this really kind woman that it wasn't a real wedding. Katie had been a bridesmaid three times, a best man once and now she would be a bride. But not really. She didn't want to cry so she nodded and pointed to the dress she'd found.

"This one."

"But why not..."

Gwen shook her head and pointed. "This one."

Eileen looked confused. Katie didn't know why she needed to look confused. It was very simple. She, Katie Archer, Kate, was getting married and she needed a dress. "I really like this one. If you have it or can get it in my size."

"I think I can. Why don't you come back and we'll try it on you. Do you want a veil or something else?"

Katie shook her head. Wearing a veil would make it seem too real. She didn't want it to feel real because then it would hurt too much. She needed to be able to distance herself from the emotions of the wedding. She couldn't feel like a bride. She couldn't allow herself to believe in fairy tales.

She followed Eileen through the swinging doors and Gwen went with them. Her sister touched her back, a comforting gesture. Katie blinked and cleared her vision, but she couldn't swallow past the tightness in her throat.

Eileen, trim, neat and professional with her swinging chestnut hair, pushed through the gowns on a rack. Finally she pulled one out, her eyes lit up with happiness. "I have it."

Katie took the satiny gown from the other woman. "I should try it on."

"You definitely should. I can't wait to see it on you."

Katie stepped into the changing room and as she pulled the heavy curtain, she allowed the tears to fall. She sobbed silently into her hands and told herself this had to be the worst mistake of her life. All the other times paled in comparison.

Because she loved Cord Shaw. She loved his wit, his heart, his strength. She wouldn't give him her heart just to try to convince him to love her in return. But how could she ever walk down the aisle, join him at the front of that tent before a God she was just getting to know, and pretend she didn't care?

"Katie, are you okay?" Gwen's voice was soft outside the curtain. "Eileen is taking a call. Look, you don't have to do this to yourself."

She nodded because it was hard to form the words. Not for Cord but for Jasper Gulch. "I'm fine. I know I don't have to."

"Are you fine?"

"Yes, of course."

"Katie. Kate…"

"I'm trying on the dress, Gwen." She pulled herself together and moments later walked out of the dressing room in the satin gown with the layer skirt and the crisscross bodice.

Eileen walked back into the room. "Oh, Katie, that's beautiful on you. So many brides try to find the dress they want without thinking if it will suit their body type. You picked the perfect dress. It's absolutely gorgeous on you. The groom will drop to his knees when he sees you."

Katie highly doubted that. And if he did, she thought, he wouldn't be able to get back up. She smiled a little and felt better.

Gwen pushed her toward the full-length mirror. "Look."

"I'm looking." Katie looked in the mirror and her heart tore into little pieces. This moment should have been reserved for a real dress, a real wedding. This sense of wonder, seeing herself in a white gown, imagining her hair up, flowers in her hands, a man at her side looking at her as if she was the only woman in the world.

It should have been real. She wanted it to be real. She turned to the left and then the right, taking in the draping lines of the dress.

"It is beautiful."

Eileen stepped forward. "You're slim and we'll need to take it in a little."

She nodded in agreement. "Yes, thank you. But is it going to be possible to have it Saturday?"

"Of course." Eileen straightened the skirt, pulled a little on the shoulders and smiled. "Yes, perfect."

Katie allowed herself to agree with Eileen. After all, that's what a bride would do. She would glow as she accepted compliments. She might act a little giddy as she picked shoes and jewelry.

When Katie left the dress shop she managed a smile for Eileen...but she felt empty inside.

Cord kept the young gelding in an easy lope around the arena, holding him steady even though the horse wanted to take the bit in his mouth and run. They'd had a rocky start that morning and even though he wouldn't let his guard down, Cord was pleased. This animal was sired by Cord's best stallion and out of a mare belonging to Faith.

They might have hit on something pretty decent with the match.

A car heading his way caught his attention. He reined in the horse and turned him toward the barn. He pushed his hat down to shade his eyes and focused on the trail of dust and then the Jeep tearing its way toward the gate. The horse beneath him sidestepped a few times and Cord tightened his control, keeping the pressure of his legs on the horse's sides.

"Settle."

Black ears twitched and the horse shook his head. Cord swung off, pulled the reins over the horse's head and led him to the barn. He had just pulled off the saddle and reached for a brush when Katie walked through the door.

"Kate?"

She didn't flinch at the name, didn't question him or ask him to stop. Instead, she overturned a five-gallon bucket and sat down to watch him work. He shrugged off her silence and brushed the horse, letting the animal push into his hand a little more than he would normally let him get away with.

Finally he pushed back, forcing the horse to stand.

Katie finally spoke. "He's beautiful." Cord smiled at her from over the back of the horse.

"Thank you. We're kind of proud of him. What are you up to today?"

Katie watched him as he tossed the brush back

in the bucket and untied the horse from the cross ties. He led the animal to a stall, filled up a bucket with grain and closed the door. Katie was still watching him. He noticed the lost look in her expression and he wanted to tell her everything would work out.

"I don't know if I can do this." She shrugged as she admitted her fears.

"I know." He reached for her hand and she stood. "I shouldn't have asked. I have to admit, I have doubts about it being the best plan."

"You were out of options. I know that. It isn't about being used, Cord. You're a friend, but..." She shook her head. "I keep picturing myself walking down the aisle, standing next to you, wearing a dress that is beautiful. And it isn't real. So when I do, if I do get married someday, it will be second best. It will be something I've already done. With you."

"That's a pretty valid point," he conceded.

"I know." She smiled as they walked out of the barn into the bright autumn sunshine.

He looked down at her, at a beautiful woman with hair the color of autumn and eyes the color of spring. The breeze lifted her hair, blowing it across her cheek. She pushed it back and looked up at him, her lips strawberry and tempting. But he wouldn't be tempted. Not today. Today she needed someone to just be there for her, be her friend.

In a matter of days he would marry her. They would walk down the aisle, he in a suit and she in a white dress and they would stand with forty-nine other couples. But she wasn't really his bride. She wasn't going to leave with him at the end of that ceremony. They wouldn't fly off to Hawaii or Jamaica. He would come back to this ranch with Marci. They would go back to their routine of visiting Lulu, planning for the future, finalizing the adoption.

Katie would walk away from him at the end of the ceremony and go back to whatever life she planned for herself. He wondered if she ever thought of him in that plan. Did she ever consider that they were good together? They were good at being friends, good at supporting one another, and she felt good in his arms.

Did it ever cross her mind, the way it had crossed his, that this didn't have to end? That maybe all her intentions led here, to him?

But how did a guy say that to a woman he'd known less than a month?

Weeks before he was supposed to marry Susan, he had worried that she might not be the right one. He had been attracted to a woman he met at a rodeo in Ennis. He'd been drawn to her beauty, to her love of horses and ranching. He'd hoped she would change and be the person he needed her to be.

What a wrong way to approach a marriage, hoping the person would change to fit what he needed or wanted.

He and Katie stood at the fence. The grass was no longer green and no longer sprinkled with wildflowers. In the distance, the mountain rose up to the blue sky. Katie leaned against the fence watching his horses, smiling a little. And she looked like the perfect fit, someone he could see in his life forever. But he was asking her to marry him in a ceremony that would mean nothing.

The thing about Katie was that he wouldn't change a thing about her.

She rested her arms on the top rail of the fence and then rested her chin on her arms. Cord slipped an arm around her, pulling her close. He leaned to kiss her cheek.

"Kate, I'll find someone else. The last thing I want to do is hurt you. So don't feel guilty or worry about what you're doing to me or Jasper Gulch."

She closed her eyes and nodded.

He heard the rumble of a vehicle. He watched as the school bus came in to view and then stopped at the gate at the end of his driveway. He could hear children laughing, shouting. He watched as Marci got off the bus, waved and then ran up the driveway.

Before she got to them, she was yelling, "Katie, Katie. You're here."

Katie pushed away from the fence, swiped a finger under her eyes and smiled. Marci rushed toward them, her smile huge. Cord had been relieved that in the past week Marci had adjusted as well as she had. They'd had some tears. There were times at the nursing facility that she saw Lulu as she had been and wanted to bring her grandmother home.

But all in all she was adjusting to this new life. He was adjusting to his home not being empty. There was a housekeeper who, though not a noisy woman, was a presence, a continuous presence. Marci had added laughter and chaos to his home. The kitten was ripping apart plants and furniture.

It was good, though.

He had to catch up. Marci had hold of Katie and was dragging her toward the house, asking if she wanted to go with them to see her grammy. And did Katie want to see her room? Katie was allowing herself to be pulled along by the girl, her smile showing that she had managed to brush off whatever hurt she felt.

Or maybe that's how she dealt with life. She brushed off her hurt and moved on.

He would have followed, but it seemed his place was Grand Central today. A truck pulled up to the barn. His dad.

"Marci, you and Kate go on in. I need to talk to my dad."

Katie nodded and Marci kept talking, this time about the pizza the housekeeper made. It was the best ever. Cord shook his head and with a smile that took him by surprise he headed to the barn.

"Dad?"

Jackson Shaw walked around the front of his truck, looking a little the worse for wear. It had been a long few months, longer if they went back to the planning stages of the centennial celebration.

"Son. I thought I'd see if there is anything left to do on this wedding. You've got your fifty couples and everything else is wrapped up. Right?"

Cord shook his head. "No, not really." He leaned against the fence and his dad joined him.

"I thought you and Katie Archer were going to be the last couple."

"It isn't going to work out."

Jackson grunted. "Well, stranger things have worked out. You never know."

"I know that I can't pretend to marry this woman, Dad. It isn't fair to her."

"Maybe you ought to take a good look at what's right under your nose, son."

"What does that mean?" He guessed he knew, but he really didn't want to jump right into this conversation.

"You've had a rough time. Not just the past few

years but with Angie's death and taking on Marci. But you're not getting any younger."

"Thanks, Dad, good advice."

"It isn't just advice, it's the truth. Cord, you've struggled, but you're a man of faith. That's how we raised you. I don't think you've walked so far away you can't see that sometimes God has a very different plan from the one we have. If we get caught up in our plan and whether it goes right or wrong, we might miss out on the real plan."

Cord took a good look at his dad, surprised by the talk, one of the most honest they'd had in a while. "Dad, are you and Mom okay?"

His dad looked straight ahead, but he nodded. "We will be. I might have made a rash decision or two that she doesn't agree with. But we'll work through it. We always do. That's how we've stayed together near on forty years."

"I'm glad to hear that. We've all been a little worried."

"No need to be, not about your mother and me. But you might want to be thinking about that fiftieth couple."

"You could agree to renew your vows."

"I said them once and meant every bit of them. I don't need to say them again."

"Did you ever think about being a little romantic, Dad? Might go a long way in patching up some of the differences between you and Mom."

"I guess I could send her some flowers."

"That would be a start." Cord hid his smile.

His dad hit him with a look that effectively put the smile to rest. "Looks to me like you've been courting that little gal from Missoula. If you aren't, then you should be honest about that. If you are, then maybe you should do something about it."

"Agreed. But I'm not going to ask her to do something that might hurt her."

"That's a start." His dad inclined his head, waved goodbye and headed for his truck.

Cord glanced toward his house where he knew Marci and Katie were waiting. Kate. He smiled at the name. He smiled a lot more these days, in this past month, than he had in a long time. He wasn't foolish enough to think that he'd done all this changing on his own.

A lot of people had been praying for him. He got that.

He also knew that Katie had changed everything for him. Whatever decisions were made in the next week would change everything all over again. For better or worse.

Chapter Fourteen

Katie set up the ladder at the front of the tent where she and Faith Shaw were preparing to drape tulle as a backdrop. Pastor Ethan would stand in front. The brides and grooms would be lined up with the tulle to their backs facing him. Two diagonal lines of brides and grooms. The attendants would line up behind them, making a half circle. Katie knew from one walk-through that they would all fit. Barely, and only because not all the couples had attendants.

"Do you really think we can pull this off?" Faith asked as she handed tulle up the ladder to Katie.

"I think so." She clipped the tulle. Behind it they had made what looked like stained-glass-window shapes out of Christmas lights. Placed behind the tulle, the lights would give everything a golden sheen.

"It's beautiful," Faith offered. "You have a gift. I couldn't have envisioned this."

"You train horses and work on a ranch." Katie smiled down at her friend. "I couldn't do that."

"So we're each a part of the body, making up the whole." Ethan Johnson walked down the center to join them. "You ladies were listening to my sermon."

They shook their heads at him and he chuckled. "Need any help?"

Faith looked up at Katie, who looked around the huge tent. "We're going to wrap tulle around the support posts of the tent and then attach pretty jars of lights on some and jars of wildflowers on the others."

"Sounds perfect. If I can help."

Katie climbed down from placing the last bit of tulle. "Do you want to go plug in the lights?"

He did. She and Faith stood back to watch as the lights went on and the tulle became gauzy curtains and the lights framed everything perfectly.

"Amazing." Faith spoke breathlessly.

Ethan cleared his throat. "I think I know the ceremony by heart. Are there any adjustments?"

"None that I can think of," Katie offered. She glanced around the tent. Chairs were set up in diagonal rows facing the front center of the tent.

The chandeliers had been hung. The afternoon of the wedding the candles would be lit.

"What about the fiftieth couple?" Ethan asked as they walked toward the back of the tent.

"We haven't quite settled that situation," Katie answered without explaining. Faith shot her a look asking for more. Katie ignored the look.

"It'll all work out." Ethan pushed the door of the tent open. "Let me know if you need anything from me."

"I will." Katie remained inside the tent with Faith. It was warm inside. There were heaters placed around the edges and several at the front. "I need to turn off lights and heaters."

"Let me start on one side," Faith offered. "You know, Katie, Cord couldn't have done this without you."

"Yes, he could have. There would have been plenty of people chipping in to help."

"I don't think it would have worked out so beautifully."

"Need help in here?"

Faith and Katie both turned at the question. Cord stood at the entrance of the tent. Katie had to take a deep breath to push past her reaction to this man, to his presence. He stood there in jeans, a canvas jacket and his hat pulled low.

"I think we have it wrapped up," Faith offered. "We're turning off heaters and lights."

"You head on home, Faith. I'll help Kate wrap things up here."

"Kate?" Faith mumbled, but she turned to smile at Katie. "I'll see you tomorrow."

Katie nodded and watched as her friend left, shooting daggers at her brother on her way out.

"That went well." Cord approached, pulling off his gloves and shoving them in his pockets as he walked. "It looks great. You should think about this as a career."

"I have been thinking about it."

"I see."

She waited, wanting him to say more than that. He didn't, so she moved away. It was late and she didn't want him to say more, or to ask about the wedding.

They turned off all the heaters and then she pulled the plug on the lights that were wrapped around the support posts, leaving only the lights framed like stained-glass windows.

"Kate, I need you to believe me when I say that this wedding will work. I'll figure something out."

"You've worked hard on this. You should have fifty couples."

"It isn't really about what I want. Or what the town wants. I know that every woman wants her wedding to be special. It's all about the dress, isn't that what you told me? And your dress, the dress you always wanted to wear…"

She put a hand on his chest, "Let's not talk about that. It'll make me cry."

"When you get married, there shouldn't be another wedding, another dress or another groom in your past. Julie and Faith have both told me, and they didn't hold back, that I was wrong to ask you to do this."

"You weren't wrong. You asked a friend to help you out." A friend could do that. Couldn't she? It didn't have to hurt, not if she kept it all in perspective. She was going to put on a dress and help out a friend. It wasn't so different from her junior prom when she'd accepted the invitation from a friend because he didn't want to go alone and his girlfriend had just broken up with him. By the end of the night, he and the other girl had gotten back together and Katie had sat at the table for girls without dates. It hadn't been so bad.

Really.

"Yes, I asked a friend to help me out." He smiled as he said it. "But this is different than asking you to do some dishes or give me a ride to town. I asked you to marry me."

"I guess that does make it a little more serious. But I can do this, Cord. I have a dress already ordered. It isn't as if it will keep me from ever having a real wedding."

"No, it won't. But—"

She put a finger on his lips to stop him. "Just get a ring before I change my mind. It obviously doesn't have to be fancy. It can be out of a gumball machine if you want."

"Okay. A ring it is. And, Kate," he added, flicking a finger across her cheek where a tear had slid free, "if you change your mind, we'll still be friends."

"Of course." She smiled, but it quickly evaporated as a chill swept over her, making her shiver in the changing temperature of the tent. Obviously the heaters worked.

"Are you cold?"

"No, I'm fine." She buttoned her jacket and smiled. "There, all better. Now, time to get this place closed up and go home."

Home, funny that she considered Shaw Ranch, a place she had no connection to, her home. And the man watching her, she felt connected to him, too. But he was a friend. Just a friend.

Cord didn't know what else to say. She was willing to walk down the aisle with him. He should talk her out of it. Crazy as it seemed, he wanted to see her walk down the aisle in a white dress. He wanted to buy her a ring and slip it on her finger. He wanted to kiss her.

Hc didn't want this month to be over, because

when the month ended, he was afraid her time here would come to an end. She hadn't committed to the store. In the end, it couldn't matter for him. His life would settle into his new reality, raising Marci on his own. He had to keep his mind on what had been his priority for almost a dozen years.

He knew he would miss Kate. All the lectures to himself about how he shouldn't have gotten involved, shouldn't have let her in, were pretty useless now.

He cleared his throat and stepped away from temptation. "Let me pull the plug on the last strand of lights and we'll go. I know I'm beat and I'm sure you are, too."

"Yes." Her voice shook a little as she answered. "How is Lulu?"

"Good days and bad. Marci is the same. Good days and bad. She's excited, she's sad, quiet, talks my leg off. I know we'll get through it. But today when we visited, Lulu didn't remember Marci's name. I know it hurt her. But they sang their song."

"I'm so sorry, Cord," she said, and then her hand reached for his, drawing him to her side.

"Kate, I'm not sure why you're here, but when I think about this past month without you—" he held her a little closer to him "—I'm glad you were here."

"Shh," she whispered.

"Okay."

"Don't say anything we have to think about tomorrow."

He agreed, kissing the top of her head before he moved a step back. By next week they'd be going back to their real lives and he didn't know who she was in that real world or what she really wanted.

"We should go," he said, starting them toward their cars.

"Yes, we should. Good night, Cord."

"Kate?"

She shook her head as she backed away from him. "Not tonight."

He watched her leave, knowing he should go after her but knowing she really needed time away from him. He probably needed time, too.

In two days he would walk her down the aisle, although it wouldn't be legal since they wouldn't have a marriage license. And she was more the person he wanted to marry than either of the women he had nearly married for real.

He watched as the Jeep roared to life and took off. A truck was parked behind his, running, exhaust pouring from the back. He watched as Julie got out of the truck and walked toward him. Mad. Yes, he'd seen that look on her face before.

"For an older brother, you sure know how to make a mess of things."

"What does that mean?"

"Well, I was driving through town after a meeting for the committee planning the Thanksgiving Parade and Homecoming Feast, a meeting you were supposed to attend. I thought I'd stop by and fill you in on what we discussed."

"Oh."

"Yeah, oh. And what do I see but you and Katie. And I think you shouldn't use your very obvious charms to convince her to do this wedding. She's more fragile than she looks."

"I told her not to do the wedding, Julie."

"But for you she's going to do it anyway."

"Yes, I guess she is," he admitted.

"What in the world are you thinking, Cord? You've never been like this."

"Little sister, if I knew what I was thinking, life would be perfect. As it is, I'm pretty confused about a lot of things."

"My older brother, confused? It must be love."

He shook his head. This wasn't a conversation he was going to have with Julie. "Why did you stop by here?"

"For two reasons. First, you have to save Faith from our father's matchmaking schemes. Seriously, Wilbur from the bank?"

"He's a good guy and Faith isn't going to fall

for Dad's schemes. Maybe that's the reason Mom is upset with him. He's been pushing hard to get us all married off."

"Okay, second. Have you been able to contact any of the Masseys?"

The other founding family of Jasper Gulch. Silas had left years ago and none of them had returned since. But why would they? They had no ties to this little town. "No, I haven't. I've found some Masseys, but the ones I've called either aren't related or aren't returning my calls when I leave voice mail. As much as we'd like to have a Massey at the celebration, I don't think we will."

"Don't be gloom and doom. It will all work out. Things usually do work out, Cord. I know you've got this twice-burned issue to work through. But don't forget the other old adage, third time's the charm."

She danced away from him and hurried back to her truck.

"That's real funny," he muttered. She must have heard, because she laughed as she got in the truck and closed the door.

Third time's the charm. Was Kate his third attempt at finding the woman he'd spend his life with? Or would she walk away from him, from Jasper Gulch and from this wedding? Even though she'd said yes, he wasn't convinced her heart would let her walk down the aisle with him.

* * *

On Friday, Katie looked around the overcrowded festival hall. A hum of voices and laughter combined with the strong scent of nail polish and remover. The noise made it hard to think inside that building. And she desperately needed to think. She'd told Cord she would walk down the aisle with him. Her dress had arrived. The gown was hanging in the storage area with her name on it. Forty-nine other dresses hung on the same bar that had been installed just for the job of holding dresses.

"Katie, over here." Annette, owner of the Cutting Edge Salon, motioned her over to a chair. "Do you know what you want done with your hair tomorrow?"

"I don't have a clue."

"You should be more excited," Annette offered. And then she looked in the mirror at Katie's image and frowned. "But you're not. Any woman in her right mind marrying Cord Shaw would be ecstatic. That man is eligible and gorgeous."

"He is amazing," Katie agreed. But she wasn't sure about the eligible part of the equation. Cord might be single. He might hold her the way she thought a man should hold a woman, but she also thought he kept his feelings as tightly reined in as he kept that young horse he owned.

Cord Shaw wasn't a man who was going to make another mistake when it came to a relationship. And she understood. He had Marci and Lulu to think about. He had past scars. For Cord, Katie was a friend. She was the person doing him a favor.

"It's great that the two of you decided to get married and fill this spot." Annette lifted her hair. "I think a pretty French braid with baby's breath. I'm finding out what the women want so that I can have all our supplies here tomorrow."

"That sounds good." She looked in the mirror and tried to visualize the French braid. It hadn't been her plan, but then, neither had this wedding. So what did it really matter?

Annette leaned in. "Katie, are you and Cord doing this just to make sure we have fifty couples?"

Katie smiled up at the other woman. "Annette, I love this town."

"Yes, you do. I just hope Cord hasn't pushed you in to something…."

"Don't blame Cord for this. I'm doing what I want to do. For a friend."

"Are you really trying to convince yourself that all you feel for that man is friendship? I've been down that road. I didn't want a dog. But I got Stormy. And I sure didn't want a man. But I'm thrilled that I'll be marrying Tony." Annette shook her head, bouncing her dark hair with the neon highlights. "I'm going to give you some free beauty-shop advice."

"Oh, good."

"Don't let him go, Katie. Fight for what you want. If you love that man, show him. Don't let him think of you as just a friend. Let him see the woman that you are and don't let him get away with holding back and pretending he doesn't need you in his life."

"That's very good advice," a voice from behind them spoke softly.

Katie turned to smile at Julie. "You didn't hear that."

"Oh, yes, I did," Julie said and looked to Annette, who would obviously have a response.

"Honey, this is the beauty shop, at least for today, and this is what we do. We talk romance and forever, and how to control these wild men of ours."

Katie looked out at the group of women joined to prepare for their weddings. Olivia was getting a pedicure and laughing as the young woman painting her nails said something. Hannah Douglas looked relaxed getting a manicure. Of course she was relaxed, she was marrying the man of her dreams and for a few hours she could be pampered and not chase her twins.

Beth had returned to be her sister's bridesmaid.

She'd been making eyes at one of the Shaw men, or maybe both Adam and Austin were in the radar. Last night, she'd mentioned finding a way to get Cord Shaw to look at her, if Katie didn't mind.

Katie had smiled and decided not answering was better than admitting to something she didn't want to admit to. Not when they were in the Shaw home and at any moment a Shaw could have walked in on them. At the time, it had been just her, Beth and Ranger, the poodle.

Across the festival hall Gwen was sitting with their mother, who had barely spoken to Katie since she found out that Katie, too, would be getting married. Katie's parents had arrived that morning and were staying in Ennis, making the drive rather than staying with the Shaws.

"I came here to help my sister," she said, not to anyone in particular.

Julie leaned in to hug her. "And maybe you came here because God had other plans for you."

At that, she looked up and smiled. "Maybe so. I've learned I'm a pretty decent wedding coordinator. Let's talk about something else, because a bride, even a fake bride, shouldn't cry the day before her wedding. That can't be good luck. Julie, how is Ryan faring with all these wedding plans?"

Julie leaned close. "Don't tell, but last night he threatened to toss me in the truck and elope. We were going to drive to Coeur d'Alene, Idaho, and get married at a wedding chapel. We talked each other out of it."

"Wouldn't that be amazing!" Annette put a hand over her mouth and her eyes widened. "Oh, Julie, you're a genius. I'm getting married in Coeur d'Alene. I won't elope, though. I'll need a couple of bridesmaids."

Katie groaned and closed her eyes. Annette and Julie both laughed. This was how it felt to be a part of lives, a part of a community.

"Have you had any luck finding the time capsule?" Katie asked Julie, changing the subject back to the town.

"None at all. I'm really worried that come December we won't have the grand finale."

"You'll find it. Someone will come forward. Surely someone knows something or saw something?"

Julie shrugged. "I don't know. Dad is beside himself, worrying over it. Mom is a mess. But for now, we have to work on the Thanksgiving Parade and Homecoming Feast. I hope you'll be here for that, Katie."

"And you hope you can find a Massey to show up," Annette added, lifting Katie's hair with a thoughtful expression. "Ringlets and baby's breath?"

Katie shook her head. "No, I don't see it. I'm too tall. If I was pretty and petite, maybe."

"You're beautiful and elegant," Julie admonished with a frown. "You need to see yourself for who you are, the person we see."

Annette looked out at the crowded room. "Tomorrow this is going to be a wedding reception. I'm just amazed."

"They're putting up another tent to seat people." Katie supplied the information, glad for something new to talk about, something else to think about.

When she thought about the wedding tomorrow, she still wondered if she could go through with it. She didn't know if she could let Cord Shaw slip a ring on her finger and not have it break her heart.

Chapter Fifteen

Saturday afternoon, the brides and bridesmaids arrived at the fairgrounds, converging on the festival hall, chattering and laughing. Katie had been there for more than an hour, making sure tables were set up, decorations were taken care of and the caterers had what they needed. The brides arrived and hurried to the back room of the hall where their hair would be done if needed. The wedding dresses were also there, waiting for them.

Katie trembled on the inside, wishing she could be anywhere but here. Last night they'd had rehearsal with sandwiches and appetizers after. She'd had to walk down the aisle with other couples, meet Cord at the front of the tent, stand next to him while vows were repeated, hold his hand, kiss him at the end of the ceremony.

If last night was any sign, today would be a nightmare of emotion. But she could do this.

"Why are you doing this?" Her mother came up behind her, her eyes troubled.

Everything had been so chaotic, they hadn't really talked. Katie hadn't *wanted* to talk, to explain. Why would she pretend to get married?

"Because I want to help pull this off."

"Can't you do it without getting your own heart broken?"

The words surprised Katie. She looked at her mother, waiting to hear what a mistake she was making, a bad choice. Instead, there was understanding.

"Do you love him?"

Katie bit down on her bottom lip and blinked furiously. "Please don't make me cry. My mascara will run. I'll have a puffy face."

"Katie, I understand that you want to move here. I know you want to test your wings and find your own place in life. But this wedding and what you're doing for this man… I'm not sure if this is right."

"I know." Katie managed a watery smile. "But I'm going through with it. And I'm glad you're here."

"To see my two daughters marry the men of their dreams?" Her mother's tone was devoid of humor.

"Yes, I suppose."

"Katie, this is a mistake."

"I've made a lot of them in my life."

Her mom shook her head. "That's the trouble with you, Katie."

"No, please don't say that. I've heard it my whole life. It's my mantra, the trouble with Katie."

"That isn't what I meant."

"No, but it is what you always say. You and Dad both. It should be a book title, really. It does have a ring to it."

"Katie, you're tired and emotional and this wedding is a very bad idea. You don't walk down the aisle with a man and vow to live your life, cleaving only unto him, and then walk away to go back to your separate lives."

"We don't have a marriage license and are only standing up with the other couples, not saying the vows." She sobbed on the words and her mother touched her hand, holding it.

"Find him and tell him you can't."

Katie nodded and walked away. She joined the other brides in the back room. It was crowded, but the women were laughing and talking. The only one with tears or doubts was Katie. She avoided looking at Julie, who was in the process of letting Nadine help her slip Elaine Shaw's dress over her head.

"Here's your dress." Gwen appeared at her side holding a dress covered with plastic. "I'm going to finish getting ready, but I thought I should help you get started. You're looking a little dazed."

"I'm good."

"Mom?"

Katie nodded. "Don't worry, it wasn't bad. It was actually very sweet."

"Good. Now, get your dress on. Can't keep the groom waiting."

Katie watched her sister walk away. Their mother had entered the room. She'd looked at Katie, then at Gwen. Katie nodded, and their mother turned to Gwen. She was, after all, the real bride.

Katie pulled the cover off the dress and then she couldn't breathe, she couldn't move. She shook her head as she stared at the creation of silk she held in her hands.

"Gwen, no!" Katie felt Julie's hand on her sleeve, but she pulled away and hurried to her sister. "This is your dress."

"No, it's yours."

"You had it taken in. It fits you and you're wearing it." Katie shoved the dress at her sister. "Gwen, don't do this. I can't wear this dress."

"You've always wanted to wear it. I can't walk down the aisle in that dress and then pass it on to you. I want you to wear it and I didn't have it taken in. Don't argue."

"But I'm not getting married, we both know

that. This dress shouldn't be wasted on a wedding that isn't real, a bride that isn't a bride."

"Are you walking down the aisle to the man of your dreams?" Gwen asked, a smile on her face.

"No, I'm walking down the aisle to a man who asked me to do him a favor."

"Katie, I have a dress." Gwen held up a lacy creation. "It's more my style and my size."

Their mother pushed Katie's great-grandmother's dress back into her hands. "Wear the dress, Katie."

She held the dress against her and thought about the walk down the aisle, about Cord meeting her at the front of the tent. In her mind she heard the vows the way they'd been said the previous evening during the rehearsal. The promise to love, to cherish, to honor.

As the other brides finished getting ready, she slipped the dress over a chair and walked away.

Cord adjusted his tie and slicked down his hair with his hand. He looked around city hall at the other men in their suits. Grooms. They were all the real deal. He was an impostor.

Ryan Travers walked up and patted him on the back. "You look like a man about to get married."

"Yeah, I guess I do."

"What if you get there and she's not there?"

"I'll survive. The town will survive." What if she wasn't there?

Maybe he should be the one who backed out. He could do that. He could give her the escape she needed instead of making her be the one to back out.

"Cord," Pastor Ethan Johnson greeted him, stepping around a few of the grooms who were finishing ties and jackets.

"Ethan, looks like we're almost ready for this."

Ethan shot Ryan a look and the other man walked away, leaving Cord with the pastor. "Cord, let's take a walk."

"A walk?" Cord looked around, making a point. "Where would we walk to?"

"You know better than I do."

Cord nodded toward the door. "I guess we'll have to go outside."

"Works for me."

The two men stepped out the door and Cord took a deep breath. The fresh air did feel good. He rarely put on a suit. He couldn't really remember the last time. It itched and the collar was tight.

"Feeling a little uncomfortable?" Ethan asked with a smile.

"Yeah, I guess I am."

"Maybe you should think about what you're doing here?"

Cord looked around. He spotted the big banner stretched across the road. WELCOME TO JASPER GULCH'S CENTENNIAL CELEBRATION.

"You mean the celebration or the wedding?"

"The fact that you are about to walk down the aisle with a woman you clearly love, pretend you don't love her while I read the vows you've no intention of honoring..."

"Stop!" Cord put a hand up. "I think I get your point and I'm afraid this is going to end with you hitting me."

"Never. But I would like to knock some sense into you."

"I wish someone would," Cord admitted, brushing a pretty shaky hand through his hair.

"Then think about what you're about to do here."

"I've been thinking, Ethan. I've done so much thinking I'm about worn out from it. I'm trying to do the right thing for our town. I'm trying not to hurt Kate. I'm not sure which end is up."

"I guess I'd be remiss if I didn't ask you to pray."

"I guess you probably should have mentioned that a few weeks ago."

With that, Cord walked away, wishing God could send a text or an email because it would be nice to know, without a doubt, what he was meant to do. Katie Archer had changed his life, that much was obvious. She'd helped him through one of the toughest months of his life.

A better man than himself would head to the fairgrounds and tell her she didn't have to go through with this sham of a wedding. It'd all seemed so easy when he'd come up with the idea. They wouldn't say the vows as the other couples said them. They wouldn't have a marriage license. They would just fill a space. Not the best idea he'd ever had.

As he headed for his truck a short time later, that was the thought on his mind. He had to back out of this wedding. Katie deserved to someday walk down the aisle without memories of this fake wedding hanging over her like a cloud.

She deserved not to be used.

Cord had other duties before he could talk to Katie and tell her their wedding, fake as it might be, was off. He had to go in front of the crowd gathered in the wedding tent and thank them for coming to Jasper Gulch. He had to stand there as the media took pictures and hoped for something interesting to report.

The grooms were all in the reception tent waiting. The brides were in the festival hall. Marci was with them, putting on a pretty bridesmaid's dress Katie had helped her pick out. He had to get this speech over with so he could stop them from walking out to meet him.

He stepped to the front of the tent, clipped the lapel mic to his jacket and smiled at the gathered crowd. They clapped for a long period of time. He finally explained that the wedding would begin in fifteen minutes.

"First, I want to thank all the couples who are participating. They've made this an amazing experience. I want to thank their families. I know that we all have ideas about weddings, what we want for our loved ones. And a wedding with fifty couples usually isn't at the top of the list."

More applause. Cameras flashed as the media moved closer, taking pictures. He'd already talked to several journalists.

"I want to thank our wedding coordinators. Helen Avery helped at the beginning, but another job made it impossible for her to finish. We thank Kate Archer for taking over and for providing this amazing experience for our couples."

He lifted his gaze from his notes and saw something at the back of the church. A hand waved. Faith, wearing her bridesmaid's dress, stood in the doorway, waving her arms. He drew in a breath and continued trying to ignore her wild pantomime.

"As the wedding vows extol, marriage is not an institution to be entered into unadvisedly. When

I think of marriage, I think of Jasper Gulch, of small-town values, of people who hold on to each other through the tough times. This town has seen tough times. It has seen its share of ups and downs. The citizens of Jasper Gulch sometimes see eye to eye. Sometimes they don't. But they work it through." He glanced around the crowd and tried to remember what came next. Faith was still waving to get his attention. "The citizens of Jasper Gulch know that to keep a town united you have to keep working through the hard times. There's a foundation of faith, of love, of hope. With those three elements, a marriage is stronger. A community is stronger."

And without Katie Archer, he was weaker. Because she was his other half. His phone buzzed. He pulled it from his pocket, knowing the text would be from Faith. He smiled an apology because any other time he would have let it ring.

Hurry. Can't find Katie, it said.

He smiled at the confused-looking crowd, including his dad in the front row. "I'm sorry, I have to leave you all now. But the wedding will begin shortly."

With that, he ran down the aisle and out the side flap of the tent. Deputy Cal Calloway was pulling up as Cord made his dash to the festival hall. He stopped when the cop flashed the lights at him. Taking a deep, pretty impatient breath, he strolled over to the police car as the window came down.

"Cal, you coming to the wedding?"

"Not today, Cord."

Unease settled in his gut. "Cord, Rusty Zidek just found the time capsule. He was driving his ATV mule this way, across the fairgrounds."

Cord looked around, unsure of what to do or say next. "I should tell my dad."

"You've got a truckload of media in that tent. They're armed with cameras and recording devices. If I was you, I'd get this wedding over with and then we'll all have a good sit-down and discuss what comes next."

Cord nodded and stepped away from the car. The time capsule had been found. Too late, he thought to ask if there was anything in it. Cal had already pulled away.

He also should have asked the cop if he'd seen Katie. Faith was heading his way, but someone had walked up behind him. He turned, hoping it would be Katie. It was his dad.

"Cord?"

"Dad."

"You okay?"

"I'm good."

"You ran out of there in a hurry."

"Faith said they can't find Kate." He was already walking, leaving his dad to catch up. Faith was almost to them.

His dad nodded. "I'll help you find her. What was Cal doing here?"

"Dad, they found the time capsule. Rusty found it. We'll talk after this wedding is over. Cal is right, we don't want to rush off right now and give the media something to cover other than the wedding."

He looked off in the direction of the time capsule's location. "Well, if that don't beat all."

"Yeah. Now, if you'll excuse me. I have to find my bride."

"Find your bride?" His dad's brow furrowed, but he didn't push.

"Yes, bride. Dad, can you stall this wedding?"

"I'll give you fifteen minutes."

Cord started across the parking lot and Faith grabbed his arm. "She was pretty upset, Cord."

"About?" As soon as the word left his mouth, he knew what about. He knew because he'd been standing in front of a tent full of strangers discussing the merits of a strong relationship when he realized that over the past month, Katie had become that person for him.

In a month? She'd been the person with him as he coped with Lulu's dementia. She'd been with him as he comforted Marci. And through it all, he realized now he'd been that person for her, as well.

At the door of the festival hall they were met by Annette, who had become Katie's assistant for the day. And obviously bouncer of men trying to gain access to the brides.

"What are you doing here, Cord Shaw?"

"I need to see Kate."

"Well, I hope you can find her. She put on the dress that was her grandmother's, looked in the mirror and said she couldn't do this. Be a good boy and don't break her heart."

"I'm trying to keep from breaking her heart, Annette. Now, if you or someone else could tell me which way she went?"

"I'm sorry, Cord, I really don't know." Annette looked at Faith. "Did you happen to see?"

Faith shook her head and before she could answer, Marci was sliding through the door, wiggling her way around Annette. "She got in her Jeep."

"Which means she could be anywhere." Or gone for good. Cord brushed a hand over his face. "I guess third time isn't really all it's cracked up to be. We can't hold up the wedding. Annette, if you could get the brides together, I'll go see that the grooms are ready."

"Cord." Faith reached for his arm. He paused

midstep and smiled back at her but stopped her with a raised hand.

"Don't. I've had it all said to me twice before. I don't need to hear it a third time. After all, this wasn't even a real marriage."

But it might have been the first time he'd known for sure that he wanted forever with a woman.

Chapter Sixteen

Cord went back to the other grooms. They were gathered at the corner of the wedding tent, being lined up by the grocery store owner, Rosemary Middleton. If there was something that woman knew how to do, other than meddle, it was how to keep some men in line. The thing about Rosemary was that meddlesome or not, everyone liked her.

"Cord, we're going to have you at the back of the line. You're the last one in." She reached for his arm and he shook his head.

"No, we won't be having fifty couples today, Rosemary."

She gasped. "Oh, honey, not again."

Right, of course, that's what he'd be known for. The next centennial celebration, when he was long gone, they'd still be talking about Cord Shaw, who had been jilted three times. By then, maybe people would know that this third wedding hadn't been real. Or maybe this third time would be known as the time that turned him off romance forever.

"It happens." He smiled as he said it.

She patted his arm, "No, honey, it doesn't."

Well, in that she was right. Another thing about Rosemary Middleton, she was always right. And she didn't beat around the bush.

"Time to get this show going, Rosemary. You go on in and have a seat. I'll take it from here."

The music was starting. He saw the bridesmaids and best men going in the front door and taking their walk down the center aisle. The brides would be lined up at the side center door, opposite the grooms. Each couple would meet in the center and finish their walk to the front. He stood at the tent opening urging each groom through as his prospective bride appeared on the opposite side of the tent.

It was the longest process in the world, and by the time forty grooms had made it through the opening, he was thinking he might take off and not watch the ceremony.

The forty-fifth groom was Ryan, soon to be husband to Julie, and Cord's brother-in-law. He shook the other man's hand and wished him his best. Ryan looked a little pale but happy as he stepped through the opening.

Jack McGuire went next. On the opposite side of the tent Livvie was smiling a huge smile as her soon-to-be husband walked toward her.

A song played about loving forever. Cord watched the couples make their way to the front. Forty-nine. It was close. He started to step away, but someone moved on the other side of the tent. Late-afternoon sunlight caught the movement, shimmered in hair the color of autumn.

As he stood there in that opening, the last light of sunset shot red and gold behind her. The candlelight glowed, warming her skin.

She wore her great-grandmother's dress. The silk was warm white, and looking at her in that dress he knew, without a doubt, that he was seeing his future. In her. Everything else up to this point had been mistakes. Bullets dodged. All to get him to this day, to this woman. His.

He stepped forward, smiling, hoping she would smile back. When she did, he knew. His.

And if she would have him, he would be hers. His heart would be hers. Everything he had he would willingly place at her feet. If only she would accept the love he had for her and allow him to make this day real for them both.

They met at the center of the tent. Her hand went on his arm. He clasped it with his other hand, holding her steady. He looked down at her and smiled. "I was worried you'd left."

"I couldn't let you down," she whispered as they took slow steps toward the front of the church and Ethan with his knowing smile.

"I almost let you down, Kate."

She faltered but he kept her moving forward, his hand holding hers on the crook of his arm.

"I'm sorry?" She sniffled as she whispered.

He smiled at her. "I love you. And I really hope you love me back or I'm about to make a fool of myself."

"Cord, people are staring."

They were close to the front of the tent, her steps were slowing.

"I don't really care what people think," he leaned in to whisper. "I have to tell you something."

"Right now?" She gave the flower-strewn carpet at their feet, and then Pastor Ethan in front of them, a meaningful look.

"Yep, right now."

"We're in the middle of a very important event."

He stopped at the front of the tent, the place where the two of them were to go left and join twenty-five other couples. "I think I know that."

"Then what are you doing?"

"I'm proposing."

Her eyes widened. "Cord, you can't do this."

He had to disagree. He could. And he would.

She was his. She'd been meant for him since the beginning of time. She'd been saved for him. He'd been saved for her.

They'd finally found each other.

Cord dropped to his knee in front of her, a gorgeous rancher in a suit that made him look like an Old West cowboy. He just needed a six-shooter on his hip and a horse. He probably had both, but not here.

Katie tried to put together everything happening to her in this one very crazy moment. She looked around at the crowd watching. She saw her mother's hand go to her mouth. Nadine Shaw gasped and began to cry. Katie hoped they were happy tears.

Ten minutes earlier, she'd been in her Jeep thinking she might leave town. But she hadn't. She'd sat in front of the store she wanted to rent and thought about the choices she had. She could run. But she didn't know what she would be running to. Or she could stay in a town with people who had brought her so much happiness. She could stay and start the business that she wanted.

She could stay and wait for Cord Shaw to realize he loved her because she thought he did. She'd come back to the wedding because he was here and counting on her.

And now.

Cord Shaw had just told her he loved her. He kneeled now in front of her, on one knee. She watched as he dug around in his pocket, and she giggled a little because what else could she do as she stood in front of hundreds of people, some friends, some strangers, waiting for a moment she'd prayed for. She'd prayed for God to send the man into her life who would love her. Just like this.

She wiped at the tears streaming down her cheeks.

"Cord?"

"Give me a minute because I have to do this right." He looked out at the crowd as if he had just remembered where he was. "You see, I was going to stand next to you today, Kate, while the vows were read. But they weren't going to be our vows. And I can't do that."

A tent full of onlookers gasped and Cord smiled up at her, that smile that turned her inside out. He was turning her inside out because he loved her.

"I can't walk down that aisle without letting you know that I do love you and no matter what, I will mean those words today."

"Cord…." What did she say? Should she tell him to get up?

He reached for her hand and with his hand

trembling he slipped a diamond ring on her finger. "Kate, I'm trying to ask you to marry me."

Someone shouted that this was a wedding and they were getting married. He grinned up at her. "Marry me, Kate. Let me love you forever."

She took hold of his hand and helped him to his feet and then she placed a hand on either side of his face, pulling him down so that she could kiss him.

"Is that a yes?" he whispered close to her ear.

She nodded and leaned to wipe her eyes on his shoulder, knowing her mascara was toast. He slipped a handkerchief into her hand and she sobbed. He slayed dragons on weekends. And he carried handkerchiefs. "That is very much a yes. I love you, Cord Shaw."

Ethan cleared his throat. "Well, that was a very fine proposal. Do you two think we could carry on with the wedding now that you've gotten that out of the way?"

Cord led Katie to stand next to couple forty-nine. He held her hand throughout the entire ceremony. He repeated the vows, each and every word. Katie couldn't stop the tears that trickled down her cheeks as he slid another ring, a wedding ring, on her finger.

"I love you, Kate Archer Shaw."

"You may kiss the brides," Ethan announced

to a joyful shout from the crowd. And fifty couples kissed.

But Katie cared only about the man in her arms. The man who had just vowed to love her, cherish her and hold her forever.

As the reception ended that evening, Cord led his bride outside. The other couples were leaving on honeymoons, many of them bundling into limousines that were lined up waiting. Since he and Katie weren't legally married, they were going to make their marriage real, as soon as possible. He watched his sister and Ryan Travers jump into Ryan's truck. They were heading for the coast. Olivia and Jack, Hannah and Brody were all taking one limo to the airport.

Katie hugged her sister goodbye, Dr. Jeff, the groom, and then her parents.

He heard her tell her mother not to worry and then, "No, we won't wait longer. Mom, I love Cord and when something is right, you know."

He had known since probably the first day, but he'd fought it. He'd fought the attraction. He'd fought the way she made him feel whole. He wouldn't call it love at first sight. No, nothing that spectacular. He'd just known that she was his.

"Where are you going?" Cord's dad approached as Cord was giving Austin last-minute instructions about his horses and cattle, as well as the other animals. A cat and a dog.

His younger brother told him not to be such a worrier before he wandered off to flirt with the sister of one of the brides.

"Heading to Coeur d'Alene, Idaho," he answered his dad. "Annette recommended it. She said we can get a license and get married up there at a wedding chapel."

"You don't want to think about this?"

"Dad, I dated Susan for two years."

"That you did. But a month?"

"A month and I've never been more sure."

"I'm happy for you, Cord. Real happy. How long are you going to be gone?"

"A few days. When I get home, we'll figure out the situation with the time capsule and I'll try again to reach at least one of the Masseys. Maybe they don't want to be found."

"That could be. It isn't as if they have real roots here. Just history." Jackson stepped away for Nadine. Cord smiled at his mom and then hugged her. "Take care of Marci for me."

"You know we will. She's our first grandchild. That means something."

And then Marci was there, her hand on Katie's. He smiled at the girl who would be theirs. "So, you'll be good for Gran and Pop?"

She nodded. "I get a horse."

"You have one at my place."

She shook her head and looked up at his dad. "Pop said I get my own horse to break. Faith will help me."

"Great. Don't break an arm while I'm gone."

"I can't go?"

He shook his head. "Not on your life."

She hugged Katie for the third time. "I love you, Kate."

"I love you, Marci."

He smiled at the two of them together. Katie was whispering something to Marci. The two of them laughed. He couldn't believe how blessed he was.

"Ready to go?" he asked Katie. Everyone else had disappeared, leaving them alone. Since the proposal and the wedding, they'd had very little time alone. He had no doubt that tomorrow there would be a lot of talk about the two of them.

Katie had changed into a traveling dress and she'd repaired the mascara that had smeared during the proposal. She'd blamed him for the raccoon eyes that would be in all the photos. He'd kissed each eye and told her he loved her eyes.

And her nose. And her lips. He kissed them again, just to prove his love.

"Cord, we have to leave."

"We have to get married," he spoke softly near

her ear and was rewarded with a light shiver as he held her in his arms.

"Yes, we do."

"You might have been a beautiful bridesmaid and a gorgeous best man, Kate Archer Shaw, but you are a knockout as a bride."

"You'rc not so bad yourself."

He helped her into the truck and kissed her again before he closed the door.

Katie leaned back in the seat of the truck and closed her eyes. She was married. No, she wasn't married. Her dress was on a hanger in the back-seat of the truck, along with the bags that had been packed compliments of Faith and Annette who had raced to the Shaw ranch to gather up what they could for Cord and Katie. She wasn't married but she would be, soon.

She waited for Cord to get in the truck and then she smiled at him, feeling more sure of herself when he smiled back. This was real. It wasn't a dream. On Monday she would be Mrs. Cord Shaw. Faith and Annette were following behind them, to be witnesses and help make arrangements.

"What happened?" She meant to him, to make him want this between them.

In the dark cab of the truck he reached for her hand.

"I was telling all those people about love, marriage and community. As I talked, I realized that you are everything to me. You're the person who makes me stronger. And I hope I'm that person for you, Kate."

"I wouldn't be here if you weren't."

He grinned at that. "I love you. I know we haven't had a lot of time together. This is probably the craziest thing either of us has ever done, but I want you to know I'm going to devote myself to you, to our children and to this marriage."

She closed her eyes at those words that sounded so very much like wedding vows. "I promise to devote myself to you, Cord, to our children, to this marriage. And to God, who brought us together."

"I wish I could kiss the bride a second time."

She opened her eyes and smiled at him. "You can, soon."

They were married Monday afternoon in a pretty, white-sided wedding chapel that sat in the woods at the edge of the lake. Katie held Cord's hand as the sun sparkled through the windows, revealing a beautiful afternoon in the mountains of Idaho, the lake shimmering as a soft breeze blew across the surface. Across the way, the mountains were hazy and dark with bright blue sky behind.

This time there were no fifty couples, no crowds of people. It was just the two of them, the minister, his wife, Annette and Faith. Faith stood next to her, holding a bouquet of white roses.

The minister held the Bible in his hands and smiled at them, intoning vows that held to a sacred belief that marriage was forever. He asked them to promise to keep those vows, to cherish one another, to love each other well.

Cord smiled down at her and when the time came, he repeated the words the minister had asked him to repeat. And then it was Katie's turn.

She held Cord's hands and repeated the vows for the second time in forty-eight hours. That she would love him, forsaking all others, cleave only unto him.

And for the second time, a minister pronounced them man and wife. For the second time, a minister told Cord to kiss his bride. Katie accepted that kiss, loving the firmness of his lips against hers, the way his hand lingered on her back, holding her close, and then the way he whispered that she was meant for him. This time they were truly husband and wife.

Once upon a time, she had thought she had to chase after love, looking for someone to love her back. And the whole time that man already was. He'd been waiting for her even though he hadn't known.

* * * * *

If you liked this BIG SKY CENTENNIAL *novel, watch for the next book,*
HIS MONTANA HOMECOMING
by Jenna Mindel,
available November 2014

And don't miss a single story in the BIG SKY CENTENNIAL *miniseries:*

Book #1: HER MONTANA COWBOY
by Valerie Hansen
Book #2: HIS MONTANA SWEETHEART
by Ruth Logan Herne
Book #3: HER MONTANA TWINS
by Carolyne Aarsen
Book #4: HIS MONTANA BRIDE
by Brenda Minton
Book #5: HIS MONTANA HOMECOMING
by Jenna Mindel
Book #6: HER MONTANA CHRISTMAS
by Arlene James

Dear Reader,

It was a pleasure for me to get the opportunity to work on this continuity series. I hope that you'll enjoy it and the other books in Big Sky Centennial as much as I did. I also hope it will give you the same desire to visit Montana that it gave me. By the end of the series I was ready to move to Jasper Gulch! In *His Montana Bride,* our hero, Cord Shaw, has had to work through faith that was shaken—but not lost. It happens. We face tragedies or difficulties and we can't wrap our mind around the situation or figure out how God could allow them to happen. Afterward, we can look back and see God at work in our lives. We can see how our faith grew. We can see that the outcome led us onto new paths. And God never left us. I hope you enjoy all of the Big Sky books and that you can look at the mountains in your life and know that God has not left you alone.

Brenda Minton

Questions for Discussion

1. Katie Archer seems to be a strong person and yet she is in Jasper Gulch for her sister, Gwen, and even remains in Jasper Gulch for her. What do you think about these two opposing sides of her personality?

2. What reasons do you see for Katie's sense of inferiority and is that who God wants her to be?

3. What is the relationship between Katie and her sister at the beginning of the book? Have you ever experienced tense relations with a sibling? Did anything happen to change that?

4. Cord Shaw is the oldest brother of the Shaw children. He is strong and a caretaker. Does a man with a solid foundation of faith simply walk away from God or is he questioning and finding answers?

5. Katie wasn't raised in church, but she is searching. What is she hoping to find in Jasper Gulch? How does faith change her life and has it changed your life?

6. Why did Katie make the decision not to date? Did you think that was a wise decision for her? Why or why not?

7. Cord has had two broken engagements. He also lost a friend in a tragic accident. How did these situations change his life and faith? Have you encountered a big change that altered your own life?

8. Katie is obviously attracted to Cord. What reasons does she have for avoiding or ignoring that attraction?

9. How does Katie's presence make a difference in Marci's life? How do you think their relationship will change over time?

10. When something shifts the path we're on, such as Cord's two broken engagements, we often see them as something that has happened *to* us. How can we see that it might be something that hurts but that it happened *for* us? How was it best for Cord?

11. How did Katie's sister, Gwen, change toward Katie? What made the big difference in their relationship? Have you experienced relationships that changed as you grew in your faith?

12. Katie has to make a decision about the wedding and her participation as one of the couples. Why would this be something she really has to think about? Have you faced a decision that made you question how it would affect your faith?

13. When does Cord really begin to see Katie as someone he could spend his life with?

14. How does Katie's coming to Jasper Gulch change her life and Cord's? Have you ever made a change and then realized it was meant to be?